HENRY AND MIRANDA

CALIXTO FLORES

ISBN 978-0-9975850-2-5

Cover, photography, and design by Calixto Flores.

For mom, who assumes everything I do is great.

For my wife, who assumes everything I do can be better.

CONTENTS

HENRY

WHEN HENRY RETURNED HOME, some six weeks later, the house was empty.

After their last phone conversation, he expected nothing less. Still, EVERYTHING was gone. Not one dry cleaning hanger left in a closet, not one packet of fast food hot sauce left in the kitchen fridge.

The place, devoid of any indication of who lived there—who used to live there—felt dead. It was as if it had been abandoned before anyone had lived there at all.

MIRANDA

MIRANDA was finally on her way home from work.

She had been temping at Klaas Scherer LLC in the city for 13 months. The filing work she was doing there was tedious, but the pay was decent. And, because she'd been working continuously, Miranda was able to qualify for the temp agency's benefits plan, so she could once again afford medical, dental, and a little bit for 401(k). Medical was her biggest worry—she'd seen two friends without insurance run up huge debts after having health issues.

Klaas Scherer's offices were right on Market Street, about 50 feet from Montgomery BART, which was great. What was not so great was commuting back to Richmond in the fall and wintertime, when the sun disappeared by 5 p.m. Miranda didn't feel unsafe as long as she traveled with the rush hour crowd, but she didn't like arriving any later than 8— when ridership to Richmond station dropped into single digits.

MADELINE

MADELINE WAITED on a Bay Area train platform, the near-entirety of her teenage world packed into one overstuffed duffel bag and one (also overstuffed) messenger bag. She waited alone because Aaron—who was supposed to be there—had bailed. Or, flaked. Or, whatever. Her brother would have said that Aaron had been a wuss, which is how he referred to most of Madeline's male friends, and waiting for the train now, by herself, she betrayed for the first time that her brother just might be right.

Aaron, who was—or maybe now who had been—Madeline's closest friend since middle school, who had plotted and planned and dreamed of getting away to Seattle along with Madeline since their sophomore year in high school, had by degrees gone from being her future Seattle roommate to her train trip traveling companion to her train platform waiting buddy. Now, a no show at the train station, he wasn't even that.

Alone at the station, Madeline willed herself to stay mad—at her best friend's absence on the foggy Amtrak platform; at her parents for not understanding her reasons for leaving; at her brother for being aloof about her moving away. Being mad was the only thing keeping her from bursting out in tears over the enormity of what she was doing—moving out on her own and vowing, in perhaps her final argument with her parents, to never come back. After all the yelling and not crying she had done with her mom and dad, she was definitely not going to cry now. She had burned her bridges here, and when she arrived at her new world she would burn her ships too, or something like that. There was no way she was going to make it if stupid Aaron not coming to say goodbye was all it took to bring her to tears.

It was then that her brother showed up, walking to her on the train platform.

Seeing his little sister standing by herself, Madeline's brother said nothing about her wuss friends abandoning her, or how moving 800 miles and two states away to go to a community college was a dumb idea. Instead, he gave her an Amtrak envelope and told Madeline that their dad had bought her a ticket for a mini-sleeper room so that she wouldn't have to spend 23 hours in coach (and her meals would be included). He told her that their mom wanted Madeline to always keep her phone on, and to always respond to their family's text messages, and to ask for help if she needed it, and that she could always come back home. Madeline's brother told her that he'd come up to Seattle to check it out after she got settled and he could get some time off of work.

He told her all these things as the train pulled into the station, and he carried her overstuffed duffel as they walked the length of the train from the coach cars to the sleepers. And, Madeline, who could no longer be angry at her mom, or dad, or brother—she was still mad at Aaron, but had forgotten that for the moment—managed to board her train to Seattle without crying, but just barely.

Seattle

DALLAS WAITS IN WALGREENS at a line which is short but moving slowly. At the one open register a Nigerian-American shift supervisor is training a newly hired cashier from Lesotho. Both from Africa, their home countries, 3000 miles apart, share little in common save English as a second language. The 34-year-old supervisor's accented English is quite good; the 22-year-old's is good, but not confident.

Three high school boys at the register—Latino, Asian, Caucasian, all members of their school's nerd clique—finish up their transaction. Between them they buy one 24-ounce soda and one 13-ounce bag of tortilla chips which they will now share on their walk home from school. The young woman from Lesotho gives them their change, counting back the amounts softly. "Thank you," she finishes.

"Ask them if they would like a bag," the Nigerian woman says.

"Would you like a bag?" the young woman adds weakly.

"Naw, that's cool," says the boy who paid. He holds up the soda bottle in a gesture of goodwill—almost a salute—to the cashier-in-training. "Thanks!"

The store manager, brought to California from Guangdong province when he was three, is busy in the photo department helping an older couple vacationing from the Midwest. The couple have been taking travel photos with their smartphone which has almost run out of storage space—the husband wants to make prints of the photos so he can delete them from the phone. An affable pair, the couple remind the manager of his own adoptive parents.

The line, growing longer but still moving slowly, does not bother the elderly Russian woman who responds to the young cashier's soft "Next please." The old woman reaches the register and rummages through her handbag to produce an empty pack of Camels. "*Сигарета* (sigareta)," she says pointing with the pack to the shelves of cigarettes and computer memory sticks behind the counter. "Two cartons."

"I'll get them," the shift supervisor says. The young woman from the land of the people that speak Sesotho, left to stand at the register, half-smiles briefly at the Russian woman then looks down, adrift, at her own hands resting on the counter.

The Russian woman, two-and-a-half decades in the United States at her daughter's behest—"Come see your granddaughter, mama"—remembers first coming to this country. Despite all that her daughter told her, the then-middle-aged woman was unprepared for how shockingly different America was. There was an overabundance in quantity and variety of everything: stores, people, magazines, restaurants, churches, TV channels, phone companies, peanut butter brands—everything. It was overwhelming.

The store manager, still working with the Oklahoma couple, observes the new cashier. He sees a smart young person who needs to be more at ease interacting with customers. He does not see someone in a foreign land ten weeks removed from their life before, lost and terribly homesick.

The Russian woman sees it.

Receiving the last of her change, the elderly woman clasps the young cashier's hand. Startled, the cashier looks up to see the woman peering at her intently. "You are new in this country, yes?" asks the Russian woman.

The woman from Lesotho hesitates before answering. She nods. ("Yes.")

"This is not your home… yet." The old woman squeezes the cashier's hand before releasing it. "Wait a little longer. You will like it here, I promise."

The young woman brightens. "Yes. Thank you."

"Ask her if she would like a bag," the shift supervisor interjects.

"Would you like a bag?"

The Russian woman puts away her pocketbook. "Please, two bags."

Finished with her transaction, the Russian woman takes her double-bagged purchases and leaves. The cashier-in-training calls Dallas to the register. "Next please," she says, a little more confidently.

.

The Oklahoma couple, having had their photos transferred to 'the cloud' by the Walgreens store manager, give a printout of the photo album link to their son, who they are visiting, to share via email with the rest of their family. He edits one of their photos, his favorite of his parents' trip thus far, to post online.

Favorite of his parents' trip

Accidental and second favorite

TODAY WE ARE 50

"THE OLDER I GET, the stupider everyone younger than me gets."

Bill was slightly drunk.

"I think you mean 'the older you get,' " Andy returned, "the more stupid everyone younger than you becomes. And, I don't necessarily agree."

They both paused to take a drink from their beers.

Bill squinted, trying to parse how what Andy said differed in any way from what he said. He couldn't figure it out. Finally, he offered, "But, you know what I mean, right?"

"Yes, I do know what you mean."

Andy was also slightly drunk.

BEER, PART I: BUDWEISER

ANDRES WANTED TO IMPRESS.

After making a big deal of volunteering his beer connoisseurship for the office holiday party, the 21-year-old was growing convinced of one thing: He did not know anything about beer.

Actually, this was not completely true. What Andres did know about beer was this: He did not like Budweiser beer.

His father and brothers always drank Budweiser. This was because Andres' father only bought Budweiser and kept the garage refrigerator stocked with it. (Andres' mother did not allow beer to be kept in the kitchen refrigerator—she deemed it a waste of her refrigerator space.) Growing up, Andres always wanted to try what his father and older brothers were drinking out of their red-white-and-blue cans, and when he was 12 his mother finally let him.

It tasted terrible.

The look on his face must have told the whole story because everyone at the dinner table burst out laughing. Only his mother, smiling gently, did not laugh. She told him that this is what beer tasted like and all it was good for was making his father and brothers fat. After that first tasting, he would try a Budweiser every now and then, but Andres never grew to like it. By the time he went to college he gave up on Bud altogether.

The only other beer Andres was familiar with was Heineken, and that is what he was originally going to bring to the party. But, now he wasn't so sure.

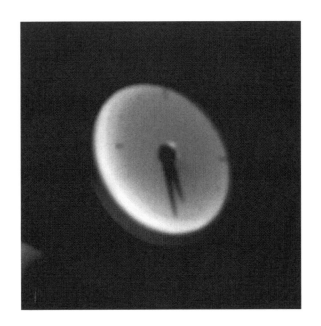

CLOCKS

Not trouble waking up on time—she woke every workday morning at 5:29 a.m., a minute before the alarm clock. Miranda's trouble was waking up to her quiet, one-bedroom Richmond apartment. It reminded her that life was now different, and that she was there alone.

Without her daughters, or Ethel the dog, or Miranda's amicably estranged husband, the place was too still. In their old San Francisco apartment, when everyone had finally settled down for the night, the grandfather clock occupying the hallway would assert itself, tick-tocking over the quiet. The timepiece, too big in their too-small home, had belonged to Miranda's parents—her mother insisted Miranda take it with her to the Bay Area. The 'tock' sound especially, beating mechanically from the hallway, used to annoy her. Now, among everything else, she noticed its absence.

The clock, her husband, Ethel, and the girls were now all in Fresno, returned there after vacating their cramped Mission Street home. Split between Northern and Southern California, they would only rejoin in a few varied, incomplete combinations. It was unlikely that they would all live in the same place at the same time again.

But, Miranda's daughters would be coming up to be with her—at least for a weekend. They were off from school and Klaas Scherer LLC would be closed for the holiday—a rare confluence of events that would give her time to take the girls into the city, which Miranda knew they missed. They would go to Golden Gate Park to look at the bison and the Ferry Building Market where everything was too expensive. They would visit The Pirate Store which both girls loved (for different reasons) and their old school so that Sister Maria could quiz the girls on how they were doing.

She would pick up her daughters at the train station in two days, on Thursday night, and for a weekend the quiet apartment would come to life. But, for now, Miranda woke up, in the silent minute before the alarm clock, on her own.

Ferry Building Market

THE TREE

HENRY WAS STUCK. For the last day-and-a-half he'd sat on the floor staring at a blank living room wall. In those 36 hours the world had kept turning, orbiting the sun, circuiting around the galaxy, accelerating away from the center of the universe. But, Henry had gone exactly nowhere.

Doing something—anything—had to be better than this.

Henry went outside and sat in the car. Eventually he put the key in the ignition and drove away. By reflex he headed a couple of blocks over to Lake Merritt, past the Alameda County courthouse onto Lakeside Drive, then past where the Cathedral of Saint Frances de Sales used to stand. Henry wasn't Catholic or even remotely religious, but he had liked the building—it had been haunting and beautiful when lit up at night.

Eventually he found himself on 580 heading south out of Oakland, then east out of Alameda County. Past Dublin, Livermore, the wind turbines on the Altamont Pass—Henry drove away from the Bay Area into the night. He was moving again, but still going nowhere.

580 split and then stopped heading east at the old 99 highway. 99 ran north-south through the Central Valley from Red Bluff, where Henry had never been, to Bakersfield, where Henry had been once and had been unimpressed.

He recalled—from the PBS show with the guy that went all around California—that there was a spot on 99 that was at the center of the state. At that spot, on the highway median, there was a pine tree and a palm tree. The pine and the palm, just a few feet away from each other, stood at the otherwise unseen divide between Northern and Southern California. That sounded like something to see, so Henry headed south.

Unfortunately, it was pitch black on the highway, and Henry was getting tired. (When was the last time he'd eaten or slept? Two days? Three?) The roadway started to swim in and out of focus, and it became hard for Henry to distinguish freeway signs from oleander bushes from overpass supports. He never did notice the pine tree and palm tree at the middle of California, if they were actually there or not.

When Henry woke up, the sun was high in the sky, and he was parked, somewhat crooked, in the vacant parking lot of what appeared to be a failed home improvement warehouse store. A bland, commercial real estate sign—"FOR LEASE 130,000 SQ. FT."—indicated that this business was no longer serving customers' home improvement dreams. A lack of broken windows and graffiti suggested that the closure had been recent.

Henry had no recollection of pulling off of 99 for a break, and glancing around at the fallow farmland surrounding the building and parking lot, could not actually tell which way the highway was or what town he was in.

Through the windshield, two rows away in the empty lot, a small tree was growing. It would have been planted by the business developer to provide the semblance of shade for the cars in the parking lot, but the amount of earth that had been allotted to it gave Henry little hope that the tree could grow much bigger. He wondered if it would survive, isolated as it was in a sea of asphalt.

Did trees need other trees? The pine and palm on Highway 99 had each other, at least. Henry stared through the windshield, and tried to imagine the future of this lone tree in the middle of a disused parking lot somewhere in the Central Valley.

Alameda County Courthouse

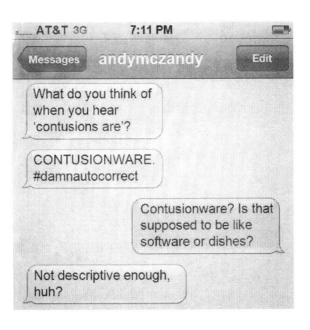

CONTUSIONWARE

ANDY WAS THE KIND OF DESIGNER who'd burst breathlessly into your office with a layout hot off the color printer. He'd hold it up in front of your face and ask, "Quick! What's the first thing you see?" Nine times out of ten you wouldn't see what he'd wanted you to, and Andy would grumble, turn around and head back to his desk.

Andy had already left the office for the day, but was still trying out ideas on Bill via instant message.

[IN TEXT BUBBLE] andymczandy —> "What do you think of when you hear 'contusions are'?

"CONTUSIONWARE. #damnautocorrect"

Blilabbo —> "Contusionware? Is that supposed to be like software or dishes?"

andymczandy —> "Not descriptive enough, huh?"

Andy was a true creative type, with sketchbooks full of notes and drawings. He was always designing or redesigning something. Bill admired this—even though it made every conversation with Andy into a mini design session. If you asked him about a TV show, Andy would comment on the sets or the title design or maybe the wardrobe, never the plot.

Blilabbo —> " 'Contusion' is descriptive, but what's this company or product? Who's the client?"

andymczandy —> "No client. I just came up with a logo for it that I think is pretty cool."

Blilabbo —> "This I have to see."

andymczandy —> "I'll show it to you over at Kate's."

'Kate's' was Kate O'Brien's, an Irish pub a couple of blocks over from the office. A good spot for hashing out ideas on the backs of napkins. The two arranged to meet over pints to explore possible markets for the as-yet-nonexistent Contusionware company/product.

Bill headed to Kate's and stayed till well after midnight, but never got to see Andy's logo design. Their IM exchange was the last anyone ever heard from him—after that Andy simply disappeared.

WE ARE ALL OF US ALONE,
TRAVELING TOGETHER

LIKE MOST WEEKDAY COMMUTERS, Miranda had developed a routine. She knew what time to leave her Richmond apartment for the BART station and how much parking would be available when she got there. After parking her car, walking into the station, passing through the fare gates, and walking upstairs to the platform, Miranda could expect a nine-car, San Francisco-Daly City train within a minute or two.

She would walk down to the far end of the platform, where the lead car would arrive. On this particular train, the lead car had been refurbished with new flooring and upholstery, and for almost half-a-year had had a new car smell. Miranda would take a seat in the front half of the car, a row or two away from the doors.

It had only taken a week for the routine to emerge, and another two weeks for Miranda's timing, platform, car, and seating choices to solidify. She had not set out to create a commuting pattern; it had grown out of a sort of efficiency and lack of permutations that came from living alone. Without her husband, the girls, or Ethel to make demands on her time, Miranda's days, or, at least her weekday mornings, had become more streamlined. More regular.

What Miranda came to notice, as her BART routine emerged, is that other passengers had routines, too. They arrived at their stations at the same time on the same days, stood on the platform at the same place for the same car, and boarded through the same doors for the same seats.

Today, she recognized two of the regulars who boarded the train at El Cerrito del Norte, the station after Richmond. The young woman and the middle-aged man, as usual, boarded from the far end of the platform and sat near the doors in the forward half of the car.

The young woman was an expert commuter. Her trip was 31 minutes long.

On this morning, like most mornings, she read and sent email and text messages and updated a few social network statuses while listening to music and part of an audiobook chapter. Five minutes before her stop, she checked her hair and outfit and deftly applied makeup, completing everything with a minute to spare. She took a moment, as the train pulled into the Embarcadero station, to ponder how her day might go.

The man was an expert commuter. His trip was 31 minutes long.

On this morning, like most mornings, he slept.

As the train doors opened, the young woman stood up to continue her passage to work. Waiting to enter the flow of people streaming out through the door, she looked across the aisle and caught Miranda's eye.

Miranda smiled. And, the young woman smiled back.

The young woman took a step for the door, then turned back to see the man, who normally also exited at Embarcadero, still dozing. She stepped towards him and touched his shoulder lightly.

"Sir, we're at Embarcadero."

His eyes snapped open. "Shit!" he said, standing up quickly. He followed the young woman out of the car onto the train platform.

Miranda could just make out the man saying, "Thanks for waking me up," and the young woman replying, "No problem whatsoever," before the train doors slid shut. The two joined and were separated, by the crowd heading towards the escalators and stairs leading up to the station concourse.

From end of the line to end of the line, commuters moved in and out of the train to and from their various destinations. Everyone was on their own path, converging briefly, daily.

An expert commuter

ON HOLIDAYS, when their extended family would get together, Andres'
uncle would always bring Heineken. Compared to the bright aluminum
Bud cans Andres saw every day at the dinner table, Heineken's green
glass bottles were sophisticated; foreign. That Budweiser was as foreign a
word as Heineken never occurred to him—its German roots did not grant
Budweiser any Europeaness whatsoever. Bud was Bud; you could drink
it when you were eating macaroni and cheese. Heineken was special and
seemingly so rare that Andres' uncle would only bring six bottles, all of
which he drank himself.

The day after Andres moved into his first apartment his father called
and asked him what kind of beer he wanted for the refrigerator. "You have
your own house now," his father told him, "You should have something for
yourself and for visitors." That Andres was not of legal drinking age was
not an issue. That his apartment should have beer in the refrigerator was.

Andres asked for Heineken. In bottles.

"Like your uncle, huh?" his father asked, answering the question at
the same time. "Okay."

That evening, after he got off work, Andres' father brought
foodstuffs for the new apartment.

From Andres' mother came 20 frozen empanadas and a big glass
baking dish of *lomo saltado* (the French fries and rice were in two other
baking dishes). "Eat the saltado this week," his father said. "Keep the
dishes for your kitchen."

From his father came a 48-pack of Top Ramen noodles. Andres
had been introduced to Top Ramen while living with his two-years-older
cousin who attended, and had an apartment near, San Francisco State

University. When Andres was also accepted to SFSU, he went to live with his cousin, who gave him lessons in cheap college living.

Andres' father set the cardboard display case of noodles on the counter. "Your mother doesn't like these, but I know you don't cook a lot. Eat these instead of wasting your money all the time on hamburgers."

His father brought in a case of beer. He set the green cardboard box, with its distinctive type and red star, on the counter. "Heineken - Imported Premium Lager - 24 bottles," it read. "Beer for you," his father said nodding. Then, he set next to it a smaller, red paperboard box: "Budweiser - King of Beers - 24 cans."

"For when your brothers come to visit," Andres' father explained.

Over the following months and years, it was his father more than anyone, that drank—and replenished—the Budweiser in Andres' refrigerator. And it was here, with his father in the kitchen of his one-bedroom apartment, that Andres came to appreciate what it was to sit with someone and share a beer.

For the holidays

MIRANDA ARRIVED at the Amtrak station early.

She didn't walk up to the train platform right away, choosing to sit downstairs in the brown and gray pedestrian walkway that connected Amtrak and BART. Months ago, when she had first asked a BART employee where the Central Valley trains came in, he pointed her to a stairway that led up to Amtrak's platform. "Yup. BART and Amtrak meet right here," he offered. "It's almost like they planned it this way!"

Miranda sat on the smooth concrete benches opposite the Amtrak stairs, a spot usually occupied by evangelicals who would stand (the younger ones) or sit (the older ones) while holding copies of *The Watchtower*. At this hour, the reverent in their Sunday clothes had gone, giving panhandlers more room to hawk their cheap BART tickets or stories of needing just 25 cents so they could get back home.

Up on the Amtrak platform the beggars had different pleas, asking for the four dollars that they were short of for a train ticket to Sacramento or simply money for something to eat. She didn't have money to spare, but Miranda would share her food if she felt the person needed it.

She walked up the stairway to where the train would arrive. There were no Amtrak staff at Richmond, but there were other people waiting for trains, so Miranda wouldn't be on the platform alone. Her girls' train would be arriving around 7 p.m., after the sun had gone down, but for now Miranda could catch a few minutes of the sunset, which did nothing to warm the exposed platform but was pretty to look at.

THE SAAPULOA GIRAFFE FAMILY

MIA SAAPULOA LOVED GIRAFFES.

The first one she ever saw was outside a hotel on the way to the doctor. Her father drove past the giraffe whenever Mia had a hospital stay or visit. It was a life-sized sculpture of an adult giraffe, and Mia imagined it walking around outside the hotel, eating unattended lunches off of people's balconies and watching TV through the sliding glass patio doors.

.

There was something fascinating to Mia about the way giraffes moved—her dad tried to explain to her that they walked by moving both left legs at the same time and then both right legs at the same time. She didn't understand, so he bent over, planted his hands on the floor and showed her.

"Left-left," he said, walking his left arm and left leg forward. Then his right arm and leg, "Right-right."

Mia stared, then laughed as her father walked, giraffe-style, back and forth in front of her. Her two older brothers and sister joined in, temporarily conducting a giraffe parade in the living room. "Left-left, right-right!" Everyone laughed, including their mom, sitting on the couch with the cat.

Mia's father tried to coax his wife to join them. "Come on, Mama!"

She declined. "I'm not like a giraffe, I'm like the cat."

Mia's oldest brother stood up. "But, Mama, cats walk that way too!"

This bit of animal locomotion information caught the rest of the family by surprise. They turned to look at the cat which had been trying (pretending?) to sleep through the racket. Now that it was the focus of attention, it briefly opened one eye, then closed it.

"Well, I'm still like the cat," Mrs. Saapuloa said. "I'm just going to sit here on the couch."

Mia's siblings resumed their giraffe-walking for their youngest sister, moving around (and in and out of) the living room. By the time they finished playing and started getting ready for dinner, everyone completely forgot to watch the cat to see if it walked like a giraffe.

.

The Saapuloa family went to the San Diego Zoo once, when Mia was still able to travel. There were hundreds of species of animal at the zoo, but of them all, Mia's father wanted his youngest daughter to see the giraffes—she had never seen one in person before.

At the giraffe enclosure, three adult giraffes moved around from one feeding station to the other taking only occasional notice of the people on the other side of the fence. Mia gawked at the animals from her perch on her father's shoulders. She watched the giraffes amble about, reaching with their long necks the acacia branches placed for them in feeders high above the ground. Captivated by the animals' gait, Mia whispered to her father, "Look, Daddy, left-left, right-right."

In the enclosure there were two giraffe calves—5– and 5-and-a-half-month-old cousins. A zoo staffer explained to the onlookers that mother giraffes didn't lie down when they delivered their babies. Giraffe calves were born—dropped really—from six feet in the air, could stand minutes after being delivered, and could run within an hour or two.

Mia's oldest brother, the tallest in their family, picked his little sister up from their father's shoulders and held her up above his head. "Now you're a baby giraffe, Mia. What do you see?"

Sticking up from the crowd around her, Mia caught the attention of one of the adult giraffe cows. Curious, the giraffe leaned out over the enclosure wall and brought its head close to the little girl.

Mia looked at the face of the mother giraffe. She looked into the animal's big long-lashed eyes and imagined that it was her mother as a giraffe and that her whole family were giraffes living in the grasslands of Africa. Mia saw herself as a giraffe calf with long legs and a long neck, standing, walking, and running just like her brothers and sister. They would spend their days eating leaves from high up on trees while being wary of lions and crocodiles.

In that instant, with Mr. and Mrs. Saapuloa holding hands and watching their youngest daughter mesmerized by an inquisitive giraffe, the family shared a near-perfect moment. It is often how Mia's parents and siblings would remember her years after she had gone.

THE U.S. POSTAL SERVICE
WILL STOP DELIVERING MAIL
ON SATURDAY

THE YOUNG MAN SEATED NEXT TO DALLAS, who was standing, was scribbling furiously in a small notebook. Dallas glanced down, expecting to glimpse Manson-esque scrawl, but was surprised. The writer's printing was monospace, crisp, regular—even in the jouncing and swaying of the BART train car.

Dallas could read the young man's writing clearly, fine black print against gray graph paper squares. He used up every bit of the notebook paper, printing neatly right from the top of the page to the bottom. His entry read:

"A woman two seats away and across the aisle is complimenting a postal worker sitting near to me. She is loud because BART is loud but she is also loud because she wants everyone to know. She says/ announces: 'I think it's a shame that the Post Office is going to stop delivering mail on Saturday. I don't think ANYONE realizes how much of a service the Post Office provides to people in this country.' She is waiting for someone to approve of her insight, but everyone is pretending that they can't hear her. iPhone screens and iPod ear buds are our excuses for keeping her separate from our individual worlds. She is trying again: 'Postal workers are like TEACHERS, underpaid and underappreciated.' The postal worker just wants to go home, I think. He is thanking the woman. I want her to stop being so loud."

Dallas stopped reading and casually looked away, but may have been found out. Neat-handwriting-guy closed up the black cover of his notebook and secured it shut with its elastic band. He didn't look up.

Dallas thought, "He's right. That woman is loud."

On BART

STOCKTON, CALIFORNIA, 1919

BILL TWEED AND OLD PADDY STOOD NEXT TO A BOXCAR parked on a railroad siding in Stockton, California. The boxcar was just one of over fifty others in a half mile-long freight train bound for Chicago.

Tweed handed Paddy a small pouch and a folded wax paper envelope. The pouch contained the last of Bill's good rolling tobacco and the envelope held three old silver dollars. Paddy pocketed the tobacco pouch and weighed the creased envelope in his right hand. Knowing what was inside, he handed the envelope back to Bill.

"You keep these buzzard dollars, Bill Tweed," Paddy said. "Don't want nor need your doc's souvenirs."

On his last short stake before reaching Stockton, Bill had hired on to clear brush for a country doctor up in Eugene City, Oregon. When the doc learned that Bill had been a stretcher-bearer during the war, he made him his assistant and kept him so even after townfolk protested being tended to by a hobo—no matter how cleaned up or skilled he might be.

Bill worked as the doctor's assistant through the winter, but come springtime was ready to take to the road again—his feet were starting to itch and he'd saved enough to make it down to California's Central Valley. On the day Tweed left, the doc gave him twelve silver dollars in a thick, wax paper envelope and bade him to return if he ever grew tired of life on the road. That had been more than a year ago, and as much as Bill had tried to hang onto them, three of the dollars were all he had left.

Paddy held the envelope out to Bill, but he would not take it back. "It's a bad road you're passin', Paddy—you hold 'dem biscuits for extry luck."

Resigned, Paddy added the envelope to his coat's inside pocket—home of his most treasured possessions. He took the bindle he was carrying and placed it through the open door of the boxcar, and with a leg up from Bill and a hand from another rider already onboard, climbed into the eastward-bound conveyance.

It would be a while before the freight train and its cargo, listed and unlisted, would begin its journey, but Bill Tweed elected to make his farewell now before heading off to camp for the night. "Stay safe on 'dem rails, Old Paddy. Railroad bulls got it in for free fellas like you an' me."

Paddy replied, "Ain't no fellers like you nor me. Ay, that's the God's truth." He paused and smiled his gap-toothed grin, "Thank God!"

.

A year-and-a-half later, two of the silver dollars returned to California in a package addressed to Bill Tweed, c/o General Delivery, U.S. Post Office, Stockton, Calif. Included in the package were a ten dollar bill and a hand-written letter. The letter read:

"November 8, 1920

"Dear Mr. Tweed,

"I hope this letter and its contents find you, as that was the wish of my dear brother, Pedrick Washburn, who you knew as Paddy.

"Pedrick came home to us last June after 30 years away, and despite the troubles between him and our father, was welcomed back without reservation. It was Father's declining health that extinguished his ire at Pedrick's leaving, and it was Father's health, as well, that reopened Pedrick's heart to him. Our father was overjoyed at Pedrick's return which allowed him to leave this realm peacefully shortly thereafter.

"Having reconciled the reasons for his leaving home so many years ago, I had hoped that Pedrick would stay on with me and my husband, John, and our children, Allen and Elizabeth. But, it was not too long after

Father's passing that Pedrick's wanderlust got the better of him and he returned to his life as Paddy, traveling the railroads from town to town, stopping in to see us for a meal and hot bath every now and again.

"My dear brother returned to us for the last time earlier this month. It was in body only, as his spirit had departed to join our father and mother. He passed away while riding the rails on his way to Chicago in company of travelers such as yourself, which consoled me in that he was not alone at the end. We arranged to have him returned to us via train so that his spirit might look down and smile. It is my understanding that some of your wandering kin accompanied Pedrick's casket on its way from Chicago, which I am sure he appreciated.

"Before leaving home for the last time, my dear brother left me the two coins enclosed with this letter and instructions on how to return them to you. He wanted you to know that he was forced to give one of your three dollars to a trainman demanding silver coins as fare from hoboes, and that it pained him to part with your property. I offered to send another silver dollar as recompense, but Pedrick said that it would not equal what had been taken. I have included a ten dollar note instead, not in exchange for your dollar that was lost, but as a token that you might use to add some comfort to your life.

"If your journeys should ever take you eastward to Missouri, please find us at the Washburn House in St. Louis. You are welcome here at the home where my brother Pedrick and your friend Paddy was born.

"Yours sincerely,

"Anna Elizabeth Washburn Wilcox

"St. Louis, Mo."

The package and its contents waited for Bill Tweed at the Stockton, California Post Office in the postmaster's bottom desk drawer for months, then years—long past the pickup deadline for general delivery mail.

MEMORY OF COFFEE GONE BAD

BILL HAD A MORNING MEETING with two up-and-coming app programmers—kids barely out of high school—and needed a couple of coffee mugs for the hospitality portion of the gathering. Usually he would grab some company mugs from the dishwasher, but no one in the office had run it the night before.

He rummaged around in the upper cupboard where clean drinkware would theoretically be and amongst the collection of mismatched glasses and cups he came across Andy's old commuter mug. The mug must have been in the dishwasher and put away in the cupboard since Andy hadn't been around to collect it and bring it back to his desk.

That Andy's mug had ever been in the dishwasher made Bill laugh to himself. As far as he could remember, the mug had always been partially full of coffee and had rarely, if ever, been washed. During the workday, overnight, even over the weekend, the commuter mug held some level of coffee that Andy would drink from whenever he picked it up next.

.

A couple of years ago, after a long holiday weekend, Andy wandered into the office kitchen where Bill was brewing a cup of tea. Andy held his commuter mug, lid off, in front of Bill's face. The mug was about a quarter full of coffee with small islands of mold floating on the liquid's surface.

"Do you think I can still drink this?" Andy was not joking. If there was even the remotest possibility that he could safely consume four-day-old mold-infused coffee, he would.

Bill cringed at the sight. "Are you insane? And, get this thing out of my face."

"What if I microwave it?"

"First of all, it's an aluminum mug. Second, if you don't move this damn thing away from my face I'm going to throw it and you out the window."

"So you're saying don't drink it." Andy stared into his mug, disappointed.

Bill took the mug and unceremoniously dumped its contents into the sink. He turned the hot water on full hoping it would kill off whatever had been taking sustenance from Andy's coffee. "I swear to God, Andy…"

.

Bill stared at the empty commuter mug, clean and dry and missing its lid. After a moment he dropped a tea bag in it and filled it with hot water from the dispenser. For the app wunderkinder Bill grabbed two company-logoed mugs out of the cupboard. He brought his tea and the two empty mugs into the conference room where coffee, water, and Bill would wait for the meeting to begin.

The office was on the fourth floor

CLOSER IS BETTER

MIRANDA'S DAUGHTERS HAD MADE THE THREE-AND-A-HALF-HOUR TRAIN TRIP from Fresno to the Bay Area twice before. The first time, Miranda had to pick them up at the larger, fully-staffed Amtrak station in Martinez, a half-hour drive away.

By the rules, Amtrak would not take unaccompanied minors to an unmanned platform like Richmond—parents were supposed to drop off and pick up their children with a station agent. But one conductor, familiar with children shuttling between parents via train, offered to let Miranda's daughters travel to and from the Richmond station. "Your older girl mentioned that you live in Richmond," the female conductor told Miranda, "would it be better to pick them up nearer to where you live?" Miranda, whose car required prayers to run almost as much as oil and gas, thanked the woman profusely.

This evening, Miranda waited on the platform with four loaves of homemade bread packed into two paper grocery bags. When the Amtrak San Joaquin pulled into the station, Miranda walked up to meet her girls as they stepped off the train with the conductor. She hugged her two children then turned to the conductor, pressing the paper bag handles into the woman's hand. "Thank you so much for taking care of my daughters," Miranda told her.

The conductor looked in the bags, and seeing what was there, smiled. She gave Miranda a hug. "You're welcome, sweetie," she said. "I put my own daughter on a train once a month to go to her father in L.A. I know what it's like to worry about your baby."

They were all home now—Miranda and her daughters in the apartment in Richmond and the Amtrak conductor in Oakland where the train crew stayed on overnights. The conductor sat in her hotel room and considered the homemade bread that she had shared with her coworkers—it was good. She texted her teenage daughter in Los Angeles to ask her how her day had been. They messaged back and forth for a while about boys and the possibility of a new smartphone.

Dusk above Richmond

BEER, PART III: JACK WARNS AGAINST BEER FOR HIPSTERS

ANDRES WAS OVERWHELMED by the beer selection at Whole
Foods Market.

Normally, he only bought beer once a month at the Lucky
supermarket near campus. Beyond that, he always bought Heineken,
bypassing without notice pretty much every other alcoholic beverage.
But here he was now, searching a refrigerator case full of microbrews
and Bavarian abbey ales for what to bring to the weekend's office
holiday party.

Andres' original beer selection for the party had been shot down
by his IT department coworker, Jack. Jack had spied Andres' name
alongside the word 'beer' on the party signup sheet in the break room. It
started simply enough several days prior, when Jack glided his office chair
over to Andres' desk.

Jack: "So, what beer are you bringing to the party?"

Andres: "I'm thinking of bringing Heineken."

Jack: (mimicking the sound of a game show buzzer) "Ehhhhhhhn!"

Jack then launched into an oration that ranged from the superiority
of small-batch craft beermakers over factory breweries to the difference
between IBUs (International Bittering Units) and EBUs (European Bittering
Units). At some point in the off-and-on two-hour lecture Jack expressed
regret that he didn't have any more bottles of his home-brewed double-
hopped IPA to contribute to the party.

Andres liked Jack—he was smart and knew his way around
computers and networking equipment. But, treading into the minefield of
those subjects where Jack considered himself an authority—like music,

pulp novels, or beer—would spark an insufferable one-way discourse.
Andres had witnessed enough of these to predict what would set Jack off.

IS SUBJECT POPULAR CULTURE, POLITICS, OR RELIGION?

YES —> LISTEN FOR A MINUTE THEN DROP OUT OF
    CONVERSATION —> END

NO —>

JACK HAS ENCYCLOPEDIC KNOWLEDGE OF THE SUBJECT?

    NO —> LISTEN FOR A MINUTE THEN DROP OUT OF
        CONVERSATION —> END

    YES —>

    OTHER PERSON MORE OF AN EXPERT?

        YES —> LISTEN FOR A MINUTE THEN DROP OUT
            OF CONVERSATION —> END

        NO —> FLOOD CONVERSATION WITH TOTAL OF
            KNOWLEDGE OF THE SUBJECT —> NEVER
            END

Trapped in Jack's beer seminar, Andres realized that the one
topic where you could have a normal dialogue with Jack was computer
technology. If the conversation was about, for instance, what had
happened to the market for netbooks, Jack could be engaging,
informative, and actually helpful. Andres would have to revise his Jack-
expert-trigger flowchart to accommodate this new insight.

At the end of it, of the 40+ lessons from the impromptu
Comparative Modern Beermaking lecture, Andres absorbed 3 things that
he would use to select beverages for the party.

One: Bring a range of beers from light (color, not calories) to dark.
Jack suggested arranging a beer 'flight' for the partygoers but Andres'
confidence in suggesting what beer anyone should drink let alone what
order they should drink it in had dropped to zero. Below zero, even.

Two: The beverage selection at a regular supermarket wasn't going to cut it. A good beer shop would be best, but most upscale grocery stores would carry an acceptable variety.

Three: Stay away from what the hipsters were drinking—PBR (Pabst Blue Ribbon). For some reason, it had become fashionable for college-educated twenty-somethings to drink beer that had been a mainstay of their blue collar parents' and grandparents' generations.

Jack said that hipsters had probably started drinking Pabst to be 'authentic,' but now it was mainly seen as another part of their culture of irony. Andres didn't quite understand what Jack was getting at, but PBR didn't sound like a beer he would like anyway.

Seeing a couple of uniquely-dressed individuals perusing Whole Foods' artisanal bread selection, Andres wondered if hipsters would ever take to drinking Budweiser—authentically or ironically. Jack would have an opinion on the matter, but Andres decided against ever bringing it up with him.

TAKING THE TRAIN TO MORDOR

MADELINE SAT IN THE DINING CAR watching the snow fall soundlessly on trees, pine cones, and boulders outside. A storm was reportedly covering half of Oregon and had stopped her train here—nowhere—about an hour south of Klamath Falls.

She had woken up in her mini sleeping compartment—what Amtrak called a roomette—just as the sun was coming up. The train was immobile and a voice on the P.A. announced that the tracks ahead were blocked by snow, resulting in red signals and stalled freight, and hopefully they'd be moving again in an hour. This first announcement had come four hours ago and had been repeated, at longer and longer intervals, a few times since.

After fully waking up, Madeline had headed to the bathrooms downstairs to wash her face and brush her teeth. She returned to the roomette to change out of her PJs and fold her bed back into the space's two opposing seats. The upper bunk bed remained out of the way against the wall.

Madeline had traveled on this train—the *Coast Starlight*—between the Bay Area and Seattle once before, with her dad. Sophomore year she and a group of her high school classmates had flown up to Seattle to attend a STEM teen leadership conference. On the return trip, Madeline had opted for a 23-hour train ride with her father over a two-hour plane flight with her class. Some of her schoolmates found her choice weird, but her best friend Aaron thought it was cool—how often did you get to travel for almost a whole day straight on a train?

Aaron had also gone to the conference, and several times during the four-day trip, he and Madeline snuck out to explore the downtown

67

area. The two made a pact, then, to move to Seattle for college, though it was only Madeline, now, heading north to the Puget Sound.

The same week as the STEM trip, Madeline's dad had been at a trade show in Vancouver, BC. With his daughter's conference and his trade show both in the Pacific Northwest, Madeline's father had wanted to arrange a train trip from Seattle for his whole family. But, his wife didn't want to spend the money to fly up, and his son had plans that weekend. In the end, only Madeline and her dad were up for a family train trip. Her father booked a full-size room on the Coast Starlight for the two of them, and Madeline tried to figure out how to cram one more outfit into her luggage for the extra day the train would take.

The full-size Coast Starlight room differed from the roomette primarily in that it was bigger and had its own sink, toilet, and shower. Having a private bathroom was convenient, but the shower left something to be desired. The toilet and shower stall were combined, to the detriment of the shower, according to her dad. He said that beyond the awkwardness of bathing in a toilet stall on a moving train, the shower had lousy water pressure. "You can give it a shot," he said, and volunteered to clear out for the Parlour car so she could have more privacy, but Madeline decided to save the adventure of on-the-rails bathing for another time.

Despite having more space, the full-size room shared the same dual-purpose design sensibility of the roomette—tables disappeared into walls, beds folded up to become sofas and chairs, and coat hooks folded flush and out of the way. Everything was compact and purpose-built. And, like the full-size room, travel in the roomette included meals, which was one of the reasons why her dad had paid a sleeper car fare for Madeline's solo trip to Seattle now. Another reason was that Madeline's mother had been uneasy with her teenage daughter traveling alone in coach, something that Madeline wouldn't hear about until much later.

After getting dressed and watching the snow fall outside for a while, Madeline headed from her roomette to the dining car for her breakfast reservation. She walked down the corridor to the sliding door connecting the sleeper to the Pacific Parlour car, through the accordion gasket between cars, then through the door into the Parlour car with its upholstered lounge chairs and wood paneled bar.

Other sleeper car passengers were having their breakfast in the Parlour car's dining area—two elderly women, a young family with a little boy and girl, and a man and woman both in dark business attire having mimosas with their breakfasts. Madeline passed by them and approached the doors to the dining car.

She entered the dining car, which was nearly full, and was greeted by one of the attendants who asked Madeline if she had a reservation. (She did.) He seated Madeline at the last open table, brought her a menu, and explained that if other diners arrived, they would be seated with her— "No empty seats in the dining car!" the attendant explained. Madeline knew this already from the trip with her dad, when they had been seated for lunch with a retired couple from Boston, and dinner with an Australian steam turbine sales rep and a backpacking photographer.

Having lunch and dinner with strangers had been fun—the elderly, retired husband and wife were funny and cute, and her dad and the man from Australia had a good time sharing Sydney and salesman stories. The photographer didn't have as much to say, but he shared a pocket album of his black-and-white photos. There were shots of the desert, oil refineries, dry canals in what looked like L.A., forest, shipyards, a glacier breaking off into the ocean. Madeline recognized some images from downtown Seattle. None of the pictures had people in them, which Madeline considered asking about, but didn't. The photos were beautiful, but kind of lonely.

On this trip, though, Madeline ended up at her table alone. Maybe because of the hour, she was the last breakfast guest in the car. As the others finished up, most went back to the sleeper cars, with only two or three heading for coach. By the time Madeline had finished her meal, she was the last diner left. She watched the snow fall outside while the crew prepped tables for lunch. The attendant stopped by every now and then to ask if she would like more coffee—"Yes"—and more water—"No."

The attendant filled Madeline's cup one more time then told her that they needed to clear all the guests out to finish preparing for lunch. "You're welcome to take the coffee back to your room or the Parlour car," he said.

Madeline apologized for lingering and headed back to the Parlour car with her coffee. Like the dining car, it had emptied out after breakfast—the elderly ladies, the couple with the young children, the businessman and woman—everyone had returned to their rooms. Madeline walked past the dining area and the bar to the lounge half of the car and settled into a burgundy-colored overstuffed chair. She took out her phone to text her dad.

"Train stuck in the snow. 4 hours!!"

And, "Had French toast in dining car for breakfast. Thanks for upgrade. XOXOM."

Madeline put the phone back in her pocket and took out her iPod touch, a going away/early birthday gift from her brother. When she had boarded the train the night before, the sleeper car attendant told her that they were testing wi-fi on the train, but only in the Parlour car. Madeline hoped that the train would be able to pick up an Internet connection out here in the wilderness and the snow.

Her iPod asked if she wanted to join the wireless network "AmtrakConnect Beta." Madeline did. After clicking through a usage agreement screen, Madeline saw the Mail app icon update to show that she had new messages. She tapped on the icon to bring up her email. The first message, sent overnight from Aaron, had the subject line, "sorry."

She opened it.

"hey maddy,

"sorry i didn't show at the station. my mom was having a bad time yesterday and it seems that of the two of you, you're able to keep it together better. on the other hand, you might've made a big scene if i was there, crying and saying you couldn't live without me. so, i decided to spare us the drama.

"my plan is still to move to seattle next year and maybe get a job throwing fish at pikes place market, so if you pick up any good fish-throwing techniques send them my way.

"i'm sure you're going to be okay up there, venturing into mordor, but keep a wary eye for signs of trouble on mt. doom and barad dûr. i know you left your set of middle earth lore behind, but you probably could use a refresher on the dangers others have faced before you. i've made a recording to help you out.

"book 1.1

"aaron"

book 1.1 in Aaron's email was a link, which Madeline tapped on. The link opened a SoundCloud.com web page titled "1.1 — a long expected party." Below the title a waveform graphic depicted a sound recording. To the left of the waveform was an orange, play-button triangle. A line of description text read, "leaving home on a perilous journey, young madeline faces an immense task. this is a record of another adventurer who traveled the same path."

Madeline dug her headphones out of her back pocket, plugged the connector into the iPod and stuck an earbud in each ear. She tapped the play button, and hearing Aaron's voice, Madeline smiled.

"Book 1. A long expected party. When Mr. Bilbo Baggins of Bag End announced that he would shortly be celebrating his eleventy-first birthday with a party of special magnificence, there was much talk and excitement in Hobbiton…"

·

Half-a-year and eight recorded chapters of The Fellowship of the Ring later, Madeline visited the observation deck on the 73rd floor of Columbia Center. It was a rare clear day for the time of year, and Mt. Rainier loomed impressively in the distance.

She texted Aaron.

"At Barad Dur. No smoke on Mt. Doom. All is well. M"

Mt. Rainier

DALLAS WAS SITTING AT THE BAR IN BRENNAN'S, finishing off a corned beef and Swiss on dark rye.

At some point in the last half hour, the widescreen above his side of the bar had switched over from basketball highlights to a golf tourney. He didn't realize it, but it was the change in commercials that caught his attention more than the change in sports—Gatorade and Kias giving way to Lipitor and Cadillacs.

Dallas ate the last of the sandwich's accompanying pickle, then pushed the plate and its uneaten payload of chips aside.

He used a napkin to wipe down the void left by his lunch plate, then opened his notebook and set it down in the space. Dallas had been trying to recall a dream he'd had the night before, and he'd remembered enough hazy details to record them.

He wrote:

"A young man, maybe 25, is standing on top of a concrete wall, looking into a river. It is a hot day on Kyūshū, the southernmost of the four main islands of Japan. There are people up and down the banks and in the river—men, women, children—all Japanese—escaping the heat. The young man is the sole foreigner—*America-jin*, *gaijin*—and he is drawing attention with his height, white-turning-red skin, and sandy blonde hair in stark contrast to the hundreds of dark-haired, brown-skinned people here. The young man strips off his t-shirt, shorts, and underwear, and jumps off the wall, 15 feet into the river. The water is cool, not cold as he had expected it to be. He swims against the river's slow current. People sitting on the concrete walls stare and chatter to each other about the naked foreigner. He hears the townspeople but ignores them. The young man has come to this small town in Japan to build bicycles—single-gear bicycles that are popular with bike messengers in San Francisco and New York. There is another reason he is in Japan, a more important one, but he willfully disregards it—the same way he doesn't hear the people on the banks talking about the gaijin in the river."

Dallas read back what he had written and wondered, "What the Hell is that about?"

He considered a third Guinness, thought better of it, and called for the tab.

Above the bar, a Cialis commercial ended before returning to golf in progress.

.

Outside, the breezy, overcast Berkeley morning had turned into a breezy, sunny Berkeley afternoon.

Dallas had biked down to Brennan's for lunch and was now faced with the tedious uphill ride back to his apartment. He considered catching the 51B bus and letting AC Transit take care of the ride up. He also considered putting off the decision for another hour by heading to Peet's for a leisurely, post-corned beef coffee.

He walked out of Brennan's, weighing bus vs. bike vs. delaying.

Before Dallas could come to a decision—he had been leaning towards coffee—he saw an old man sitting on the bench near the bike rack. The old man was hunched, wearing dark brown trousers that fit a little too loosely with the waistline a little too high. He had on a plaid shirt and a dark brown suit jacket. A white ball cap covered what little left the old man had of his hair and white, Velcro'd running shoes were more for ease of use than for activity. He had a battered brown suitcase parked in front of him and was looking at an Oakland/Alameda County map folded open to show what Dallas recognized as North Berkeley.

"Do you need some help, sir?" Dallas asked as he approached his bike, the rack, and the old man.

The old man squinted up from his map to get a look at whoever was talking to him. "No thanks, son," he said, seeing Dallas. "Just got off the Amtrak. Waiting for my ride."

Dallas hadn't noticed a train stopping at the station since he'd gone in for lunch over an hour ago. The adjacent Berkeley Amtrak station was little more than a platform, sign, and self-serve ticketing machine. The declining economy of passenger rail closed Berkeley's mission-style train station in the 1970s. The station building that once served train passengers now catered only to restaurant and bar patrons—as the Irish pub Brennan's currently and as a Chinese restaurant previously.

"How long have you been waiting out here?" Dallas asked.

"I've been around the station since about nine o'clock," the old man said.

"Does your ride know you're here?"

"Oh yes. Should be here anytime now."

Dallas wondered if that was true. Or, correct. "Mind if I share your bench?"

"Suit yourself," the old man said.

Dallas took a seat on the bench and dug his smartphone out of his pants pocket. The old man resumed studying his paper map.

After a few minutes of silence the old man turned to Dallas. "Do you have a map on that phone?" he asked.

"Sure," Dallas said. "Can I look up an address for you?" He clicked his iPhone's home button to close the photo editing app he had been experimenting with, and tapped the Maps icon to launch it.

The old man produced a bulging, letter-sized envelope. It was thick with sheets of folded up paper visible through the torn flap. He held up the face of the envelope for Dallas to read.

The envelope was addressed to Martin Smart with a street and apartment address in Chicago. The return address, a self-adhesive pre-printed label, sported an illustration of an American flag and was personalized for Mr. Ellis Kamm with an apartment address in Berkeley.

"Here." The old man pointed to the Berkeley address.

Dallas thumbed the address into his phone. The map image on the screen slid sideways, shifting from Dallas' current location at University and 3rd to Ellis Kamm's North Berkeley address. The display stopped and details drew in on the screen. Oddly, the app's red location icon was planted in the middle of a street intersection.

Dallas frowned. "This is where the map says the address is." He showed the screen to the old man. "It's not an actual address."

The old man looked at Dallas' phone. "It says it's right here."

"Well, yes," Dallas began. "But, the map isn't showing a building. This is the street address, but there's no building that has that address." Dallas checked the envelope label against the info he had plugged into the phone—they matched.

"Well, my friend lives at this address, so your phone must be wrong," the old man groused.

"Must be," concluded Dallas. He zoomed in on the map on the phone. None of the nearby addresses seemed to be the right one.

Dallas volunteered to call Ellis Kamm at his mystery address. But, the old man, who introduced himself as Marty—Martin from the envelope—said that he didn't have Ellis' number. When Dallas asked Marty how Ellis knew to pick him up at the Berkeley station, Marty responded:

"I wrote him."

"You wrote him?" asked Dallas.

.

Dallas sat with Marty for a while.

The old man told Dallas that he had written Ellis, who Marty had known since they were both 10, three months ago to let him know he was coming to California.

Marty had left Chicago two weeks ago to visit his sister and her family in Spokane. He'd spent a week-and-a-half there, then traveled by train—his whole trip had been by train—to Seattle. He'd left the Puget Sound yesterday on Amtrak's Train 11, which had arrived this morning in the Bay Area.

"I've known Ellis 75 years," Marty told Dallas. The boyhood friends had grown up together on the outskirts of Chicago and were joined at the hip throughout middle school and high school. Their paths diverged during World War II.

Marty turned 18 first, volunteered for the Army and was sent to Europe as a B-17 gunner. He was shot down twice, severely injured the second time, and celebrated V-E Day in a stateside hospital bed.

College-bound Ellis was drafted into the Navy, pegged for OCS, and went to the Solomon Islands as an ensign. He was in the ruins of Manila on V-E Day and on a destroyer off of Okinawa on V-J Day, a week after Fat Man and Little Boy were dropped on Japan.

After the war, Marty returned to Chicago, got married, worked for his wife's father, got divorced, then found a new job. He traveled a lot for work, but never flew.

Ellis reenlisted, and was stationed in Japan and then Hawaii. After the Navy, a job opportunity took Ellis to California. He worked, was promoted, then lost his job when the company was sold. He started his own company, became successful, then sold it, taking care to reward his two employees in a way that he hadn't been. He started another company. Ellis married later in life.

"The last time I saw Ellis was in 2002," Marty said. "His wife's funeral. They were only together 12 years."

Neither Marty nor Ellis had children, though Marty was close with his niece. She wrote him often, and encouraged him each time to move out to Spokane. She worried about her uncle living alone in Chicago with no close family or friends.

Marty asked Dallas about himself. Dallas said he lived in Berkeley and had been born and grown up in California. He tried to explain to Marty his job at the university as a social media coordinator, but couldn't adequately convey what that meant. In the end, Dallas said that he was in advertising, because interactive marketing communications seemed like it would require too much explanation to a person like Marty who had no smartphone, computer, or even a home phone.

Mid-afternoon turned to late-afternoon as shadows from the overpass above the train platform grew longer. Dallas suggested waiting inside Brennan's where it was warmer and they could get something to eat, but Marty insisted that he was fine. He remained unconcerned that his friend had not shown up; that he had been waiting for six hours; that afternoon would be turning to evening.

"You go on home now," Marty said. "I appreciate you keeping an old man company, but I don't need a minder."

Dallas looked at Marty and his worn, brown suitcase. How old was that case, and how many miles had it traveled, never once on a plane?

If Dallas unlocked his bike, said good bye, and rode back to his apartment, how long would the old man sit here, waiting for the result of a letter he had mailed three months ago to an address that didn't exist?

"Hey, Smarty!" a man's voice called.

Dallas looked up to see a lanky old man approaching.

"Martin, you old so-and-so," the man said as he reached Marty and Dallas. "When are you going to join the current century and get a cell phone?"

Marty stood up, stiffly, to greet Ellis, who he introduced — "Dallas, this old goat is Ellis Kamm. Ellis, this young man is Dallas, who was worried I might wander onto the train tracks, so he's spent the better part of the afternoon with me."

Dallas stood and Ellis shook his hand, thanking him for keeping an eye on Marty. Mr. Kamm had been helping a friend deal with medical issues which had cropped up in the last few days. He'd tried to reach Marty at his sister's house in Spokane, but was too late. He then contacted Amtrak to relay to Martin to wait at the Emeryville station which was staffed and had a waiting room, cafe, and restrooms.

"They gave me the message on the train," Marty revealed.

"Then why did I have to run around all over the place to find you here?" Ellis asked.

"Because I paid for a ticket to come to Berkeley, not Emeryville."

Ellis said nothing.

Marty continued, "Plus, I figured I'd give you something to worry about trying to figure out where I was."

Ellis shook his head then bent down to pick up Marty's small suitcase. "You see what I have to deal with?" he said to Dallas.

"Give me that," Marty demanded, taking back his luggage. He turned to say goodbye to Dallas, "Nice meeting you, son."

Dallas said goodbye in kind. He unlocked his bike from the rack as the two older men walked away to Ellis' car.

"Your sister and I stopped worrying about you years ago," Ellis said.

"My niece still cares," Marty replied. "She wants me to move to Spokane."

Ellis nodded. "She's a good girl."

"She is."

.

It's early evening at Peet's and Dallas is at one of the metal café tables outside. His steel commuter cup sits on the table, lid off, allowing his latte to cool down.

Dallas, like many of the people seated around him, is looking at a smartphone. He scrolls to the end of his iPhone's camera roll and taps the last photo taken—the image expands to fill the display. He studies the photo of Marty and Ellis walking away at the Berkeley Amtrak stop, then takes out his notebook to write about a man with no phone number and a man with no address and how they have remained in contact for 75 years.

Berkeley Amtrak platform

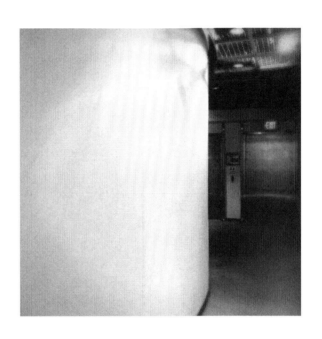

BEER, PART IV: BEER
ISN'T EVERYTHING

ANDRES WAS DISAPPOINTED.

Standing in the underlit hallway outside the office holiday party, Andres looked absently at the elevators. It had been a while since anyone had come up—at this point the tide was flowing out. People traversing the lobby now were headed down, their holiday party obligations met. Still, from inside the office, muffled music and laughter indicated the function was going well—it just hadn't turned out how Andres had hoped.

The success of the party wasn't his responsibility, of course. Andres' contribution—beer—had garnered positive comments by just about everyone who perused the 'bar' set up near the reception desk. Even self-proclaimed beer expert Jack, still chafing at Andres' declining to be taken on a Lower Nob Hill pub tour, nodded his approval at the five-bottle display of beers.

Prior to this week, Andres had only ever experienced Bud and Heinekin. But, over the last week he had spent more than a dozen hours studying beer ratings online and learning new words like 'hoppiness' and 'mouthfeel' from the issues of *Beer* magazine that Jack had lent him. From his research, Andres compiled a list of 20 candidates to choose from at the nearest upscale supermarket—another territory with which he had little familiarity. At the market he spent about an hour winnowing his list down to 5 picks: (from light to dark) Trumer Pilsner, Sierra Nevada Pale Ale, Bear Republic Racer 5, Newcastle Brown Ale, and Barney Flats Oatmeal Stout.

Now, a little more than halfway through the party, it looked like Andres would be bringing at least three cases of the beer back to his apartment. The company had catered sodas, juice, and sparkling water along with hors d'oeuvres and entrées, and the head of the office had brought two cases of wine, so there were plenty of things to drink. At the very least, Andres figured, he would have a lot of post-party beer to broaden his palate with—something Jack had been pestering him to do— even though the descriptions of IPAs and stouts did not appeal to him.

The double doors to the office opened, spilling '80s Eurodisco and a group of partygoers into the hallway. Andres surveyed the foursome as they called for the elevator to take them down to the building lobby— paralegals from the Intellectual Property division, if memory served correct. Like the last dozen folk who had crossed Andres' gaze, the group was headed downstairs to queue for the car service hired to ferry people to-and-from the party. Andres held out hope for new arrivals, though—for one in particular, at least.

The elevator doors opened. Empty. The IP staffers boarded the car, two of them laughing, one of them half-asleep and supported by the fourth.

·

The party, about an hour past its listed finish time, was reaching its actual, natural end. The caterers had cleaned up their prep station in the kitchen upstairs and packed up all the rented glassware, flatware, and dishes. Remnants of the food—pork buns, Vietnamese sandwiches, tofu spring rolls, cut-up fruit, cheeses, crackers, crudités—had been consolidated to two large platters. Likewise, the employee-contributed desserts had been combined onto as few dishes as possible.

The leftovers would be packed away in one of the refrigerators upstairs, and, beer and wine excluded, be brought out again at the start of the work week. Andres estimated that half would be consumed on Monday, and half of the remainder would go on Tuesday. Whatever was left on Tuesday evening would end up in the compost bin—the office manager was a stickler for a clean fridge.

Andres packed the remaining beer (mostly brown ale and stout) back into three of the boxes they had come in. Some of the bottles had been cooling in ice water and though Jack contended that chilled beer shouldn't be allowed to go back to room temperature, Andres didn't care. The beer would go under his desk, room temperature be damned, until he could bring the boxes back home.

The holiday party was over, and, as far as office parties went, would be deemed a success. For Andres, dejected that the person he hoped to see had not come, it was less so. His opportunity for a (pseudo-) outside-of-work encounter had gone unrealized. Perhaps a jump start on the leftovers and his cache of beer would help.

·

Miranda had spent a wonderful day in the city with her daughters. They had stayed out longer than she'd thought, and she had missed the office holiday party, but that was all right. Miranda would see the people at work again on Monday.

NEW CAMERA

MIRANDA HAD HAD A GOOD DAY.

She'd spent it in the city with her two daughters, mostly at Golden Gate Park—their favorite—and, for the first time, the de Young Museum. Her oldest girl wanted to see a black-and-white photography exhibit there, for school, and Miranda was happy to share in her daughter's interests. With her children growing up now in Fresno, she felt apart from them, especially her eldest.

She had learned, from her husband, that their 15-year-old girl had taken up photography. He'd written a few months ago that their daughter was in a photo course at school and that she had been hinting about a "real" camera for Christmas. Miranda wrote back saying to wait for their girl's birthday—she wanted to impress on her daughter that turning 16 was a milestone in responsibility. And, Miranda would be better able to afford her half of the gift in a few month's time.

After the de Young, Miranda treated the girls and herself to dinner out at a pricey hamburger restaurant in the Ferry Building. The food wasn't any more tasty than at Nation's on San Pablo, but dining with all the tourists felt like being on vacation. Her younger girl declared, "You cook better, Mama," which paradoxically made Miranda happier about the money she had spent.

They headed home from the San Francisco Ferry Building to Richmond. During the trip Miranda's little one, who had had a very long day, fell asleep in the car. After getting the girls settled in at the apartment, Miranda headed out to BART to catch a train back into the city. She had missed most of the office holiday party, but was determined to at least deliver the dessert she had signed up to bring.

The parking lot and platform at Richmond station were almost completely deserted, a consequence of the holiday, the weekend, and the late hour. Miranda boarded a five-car, Fremont-bound train, choosing the first car, as she usually did. Except for the train operator in their sealed-off booth, she had the whole car to herself.

Miranda sat down at a window seat near the middle of the car, putting the bag with her potluck contribution on the seat beside her. She put her hands in her jacket pockets and found the "camera" that her youngest girl had given her after they had left the de Young. It was a tin box with a hinged red and white lid advertising its contents— "curiously strong" peppermints. The plain bottom part of the box had been transformed with black marker into a camera face with concentric circles for a lens, a rectangular flash in the corner, and a Canon logo. It mimicked the digital camera Miranda's husband had bought for the family a couple of years ago, which their older girl was now using for her photography class.

"This is my camera, Mama," Miranda's little girl had told her while handing her the box. "You can have it."

"Thank you, my darling," as Miranda accepted the tin. "You're not using it anymore?"

"The memory is full, *y abuela*'s computer is too old to read it." Miranda's youngest was earnest. "Make sure you download the pictures first."

"I will, my love. I'll give you back your camera when I'm done using it."

"That's okay," her little one returned. "You keep it, Mama."

"She wants Dad's camera," Miranda's oldest chimed in. She added, a bit more quietly, "If there's a new camera, she thinks she can have the old one."

As her BART train pulled away from Richmond, Miranda held the mint-tin camera in her hand, imagining her 7-year-old holding it up to her eye, taking imaginary photos. What images would her little one have captured, if it had been real?

Oddly, the tin felt heavier than it should, as if there was something in it. Miranda held the box next to her ear and shook it, but heard nothing. She pressed in on the top and bottom, expecting a little give, but there was none.

She turned the tin on its side, prying it open with her thumbs. The lid was on tight, but with some effort popped open.

The box was filled with some kind of dense, rubbery foam. A solid block occupied the bottom of the tin and another block filled the top. The pieces had been cut to completely fill the box—even the rounded corners. When the tin was closed, the blocks would fit flush together, completely filling the space inside except for a rectangular cutout in the middle of the bottom piece. Nested in the cutout was some kind of memory card. The label read, "SanDisk 128MB Compact Flash®."

"Where did this come from?" Miranda wondered.

GOING BY HAND

HENRY WAS WALKING. He was outfitted for hiking, but with no destination, it just felt like he was walking.

He had left his car in the abandoned home improvement store parking lot six hours ago. The car still had gas in it, but Henry no longer needed it — the car, his cellphone, driver's license, credit cards, business cards, swipe ID, Blockbuster card — he left them all behind. Whoever found the car and assorted bits of Henry's identity could have them. "Someone else can be Henry Lee from now on," he thought.

What Henry did bring was his hiking and camping gear: tent, sleeping bag and pad, poncho, multi-tool, etc. He had a bunch of fruit and nut bars from the kitchen at the office. Someone had put a box of them out on the counter with a Post-it stuck to the side: "Bought these. Didn't like them." It had probably been Melody, one of the other programmers, who was always buying boxes of things at Costco. Henry switched out of his cross trainers and sport socks in favor of heavier socks and hiking boots. He added the sport shoes and socks to the gear in his backpack.

He'd refilled his water bottle from the two-gallon disaster preparedness water in the trunk. After riding around in the car for six months, the water had taken on the plastic flavor of its container. Henry had supposed that in a disaster, you wouldn't mind a mild plastic taste in your water, but he wasn't that enthusiastic about it now. This wasn't really a natural disaster. A personal disaster? Whatever the case, the only water he had come across since starting walking was stagnant irrigation water or ag runoff — he couldn't tell which.

Henry's walk had started off behind the vacant big box property where he'd left his car (in his mind now just 'a car.') It had adjoined an undeveloped lot which transitioned into farmland—acres and acres of farmland. He walked through fields which were just dirt, almond orchards (some healthy, one withered), thousands of earless cornstalks, and fields of what appeared to be cotton.

After four hours, a set of train tracks cut diagonally across the farmland and Henry's northbound path. He had oriented himself north for no particular reason, and now, presented with a route to follow, Henry simply did that. He walked along the tracks as they angled northeast and when the tracks coincided with a county road and turned north, Henry followed suit, walking between the disused train tracks (the rails and ties were pulled up in some places) and the road. In an hour walking alongside of the two-lane blacktop, only one car, heading north, drove by.

It was a clear and cold midafternoon, but the walking kept Henry warm.

An hour later, Henry saw the car again. It was parked, facing him, off his side of the road. The driver must have made a U-turn. Henry saw two figures as he approached. They were standing together a short distance away from the car, looking out across a plowed dirt field. One was an old man with thin, white hair. He looked like he had been a large man, once. He was skinny now, but not frail, and despite the chill, wasn't wearing a jacket. His companion, though, a middle-aged woman with dark hair, was engulfed in a big, puffy coat, zipped up from top to bottom.

When Henry first saw the car parked up ahead, he considered crossing the road to avoid an encounter, but decided that doing so would seem: 1. silly; and, 2. rude. The old man saw Henry and waved. Henry waved back.

"Hello!" the old man called out. His voice was surprisingly strong.

"Hello," Henry croaked. He realized he had not said anything out loud in five or six days. He cleared his throat and tried again, "Hello!"

"Looks like you're travelin'."

Henry shrugged as he reached the old man and stopped. "Just out walking."

"Good weather for it." The old man grinned.

Henry smiled, and shifted his pack to get moving again. Before he could take a step, the old man bade him: "Take a spell, young fella, and have a bite to eat. Elena here makes the best fried chicken." The old man gestured to the woman in the puffy coat. She smiled, Henry guessed, from the way her eyes wrinkled, since her nose and mouth were hidden by the high collar of her coat.

Henry hedged. He didn't really feel like talking to anyone, but the offer of something to eat besides Melody's rejected fruit and nut bars—Henry found that he didn't like them either—was appealing. "Thanks, I'm happy to join you."

He stood awkwardly while Elena set out folding canvas camp chairs and a table from the trunk of the car. The old man would try to reach into the trunk to pull something out and the woman would swat him away. "Put the food on the table," she told the old man, managing him.

The old man carried a big tote bag, the recycled plastic kind you get from a grocery store, out from the back seat of the car to the table. He unloaded a large, airtight, plastic container and a loaf of sliced whole wheat bread onto the folding table. "Have a sit down," the old man said, beckoning to Henry and seating himself. A roll of paper towels was the last thing to transfer from the bag to the table. The old man tore a square sheet off the roll and tucked one corner into the neck of his shirt like a bib. Henry undid his pack, set it on the ground, then sat at the table with the old man.

Elena brought a small cooler from the car trunk and set it on the ground near the table. "Water?" she asked, holding out a cold bottle of water to Henry.

"Thank you," Henry said.

Elena took out a bottle of water for herself and set it on the table. She pulled out a can of light beer, set it in front of the old man, and opened it.

"Let's eat!" the old man said. He took the lid off the plastic container, reached in, and grabbed a chicken drumstick. Elena untwist-tied the loaf of bread, reached in the bag and took out a slice which she handed to the old man. She offered the open end of the bag to Henry. He took out a slice of bread, bypassing the heel the same way the woman had.

The chicken was cold, but good.

And, Henry realized just how hungry he had become over the past several days. And, it felt like it had been a long time since anyone had talked to him. But, for some reason, or no reason, this old man was talking to him now. He said to Henry, "I'm a hundred years old this year."

Between bites of chicken and cold wheat bread and sips of light beer, the old man told Henry that he'd grown up in a tiny town in North Carolina called Pleasant Garden. At 17, he'd lied about his age in order to join the Army and fight against Kaiser Bill in World War I.

"We just called it the Great War, then. Didn't know there was going to be another one, or another three."

He was on the front lines in Europe for six months before the Army found out that he had been too young to enlist. In that time he saw not much more than mud and trenches and wounded and dead soldiers. When he was sent back to North Carolina, he decided he wanted to see something different and headed west for California.

"No highways in them days," the old man said. He looked up at some unseen aircraft marking a contrail headed east. "No airlines for regular folk, neither."

The then-young old man made his way west on foot and by hitching car, wagon, and tractor rides. He'd stop and make money by working for a week or a day, then head off again. It took him two months to reach Chicago where he fell in with another Great War veteran who introduced him to the world of unticketed freight train travel. Hopping trains, the old man crossed four states to reach Oregon's eastern border in five days, then saw the Pacific Ocean one day later.

The old man wiped his fingers and mouth on his bib/napkin, removed it, and stood up. He looked out across the unplanted field they were dining next to. "There used to be a siding here," gesturing to where the car was parked, "and, this field was all young corn. Too young to eat, but perfect for hidin' and waitin' for a freight.

"I was right here, 'bout 70 years ago, when I decided to stop wanderin'; knew where I needed to be." The old man considered Henry and his backpack. "It looks like you're wanderin' now. Someday you'll know where you need to be."

Henry sat for a moment, looking at and imagining the old man in this place as it was then. Henry wondered what prompted that 30-year-old to stop traveling.

"Thank you for the food," Henry said, getting up. He re-donned his backpack. To the woman: "The chicken was delicious." She nodded.

The old man walked up to Henry. "Take these with you, young fella." He held out his right fist, palm down. Henry put his open hand under the old man's hand. Two weighty objects dropped into Henry's palm—coins.

Henry looked at the coins—silver dollars with Lady Liberty's head on one side and an oddly-proportioned eagle on the reverse. "Are you sure?" he asked the old man.

"For luck on your journey," the old man said.

Henry pocketed the silver dollars and shook the old man's hand. He waved to Elena, who had started putting the camp chairs back in the car. She waved back.

Henry struck off north, again, walking between the side of the road and the rusted train tracks. When he looked back a few minutes later, the car, old man, and woman had gone.

Someday, almonds

FELIZ NAVIDAD

45 MINUTES AND ONE TRANSFER AWAY FROM RICHMOND, Miranda exited a Millbrae-bound BART train at Montgomery Station in San Francisco. She rode a long escalator up, past the SF Muni train platforms, to the Montgomery underground plaza. From there she walked upstairs to Market Street, which tonight was dramatically quiet for downtown, though not as deserted as the Richmond Station had been.

The office tower Klaas Scherer occupied was conveniently close to the station exit. As she reached the top of the stairs, Miranda could see into the building's brightly lit, glass-enclosed atrium, where four post-office-party staff members sat waiting. The four young women, in cocktail dresses and seated two-by-two on the lobby's red leather couches, looked ready to go home. One was leaning, eyes closed, against her seatmate.

Miranda pushed through the revolving doors to enter the building, catching the attention of the three who were awake. The young woman supporting her sleeping companion waved. "You practically missed the whole party!"

Miranda smiled back as she approached. "It's late, but I wanted to bring my dessert for anyone who's left."

A chime from the bank of lobby elevators signaled an arrival from upstairs. Miranda and the three conscious coworkers turned to see the rightmost set of doors open and a woman in a black, knee-length dress emerge. Locating the group gathered at the couches, the woman, Miss Reine, headed over.

Angela Reine was the director of patent research, one of several large departments at Klaas Scherer's San Francisco office. Nominally, she reported to the managing attorney, Mr. Jantzen, and was on the same org chart level as the other department directors. In practice, though, she influenced a good deal, if not most, of Klaas Scherer's Silicon Valley business. She and Jantzen had started the San Francisco office, the German company's first international branch, in 1985, when Reine was just 20 and working on her MBA at Stanford.

"Good evening, again, ladies," she said, reaching the group. After 24 years in California, only a hint of a clipped, German accent remained. "Good evening, Miranda."

Miss Reine was smart, stylish, and courteous, and admired, respected, and envied throughout the office. She knew the names of every one of the 212 staff working for Klaas Scherer in San Francisco, even Miranda, who was a contract employee.

Reine had come down to check on Sarah, the passed out woman, who, despite her seatmate's best efforts to wake her, had started to snore. Sarah's colleagues said they would make sure she got home safely and put to bed. Satisfied, Miss Reine added that it was not necessary to tip the car service driver since the office would take care of that.

Headlights swept across the lobby as a black Chrysler turned into the alley adjoining the building. The three staffers roused their sleeping coworker and made their farewells to Reine and Miranda as they wound through the revolving door to the car and the waiting driver outside.

Miss Reine turned to Miranda. "It's so good you could make it. I thought you and your children would have come earlier."

"Thank you so much for inviting us. The girls had a wonderful day in the city, and my little one was ready for bed when we got back to the house," Miranda explained. "I wanted to make sure I brought this." She pulled open the handles of the shopping bag she was carrying revealing the dish at the bottom. On a glass pie plate, covered with plastic wrap, was a round, caramel-colored flan.

Seeing the dessert, Reine smiled. "Shall we head up to the party?"

"Yes, but, I can't stay. I just want to bring this up."

"Ah," Miss Reine said. "You must get home to your daughters."

Miranda nodded. "Sorry, yes."

"It's hard to be apart from your children," Reine said, echoing something her mother had told her many years ago. "Sit, Miranda. I'll take your dish up to the office, and you wait for the next car to take you back to Richmond."

"Oh, no, I'll take BART."

"Nonsense, the trains are running on weekend schedule. BART will take you more than an hour to get home." Reine sat down with the expectation that Miranda would do the same.

Defeated, Miranda sat. "Thank you again for the invitation to the party. And, for arranging transportation."

"It's the least the company can do for the staff," Reine returned. She paused for a moment before continuing. "You've been on contract with us for almost 14 months, yes?"

Miranda nodded amiably.

Miss Reine continued. "Mrs. Kidwell, who you've been filling in for, has decided not to return from maternity leave. She wants to be with her child until he's ready to go to school."

"Oh," Miranda said.

"We'll miss Mrs. Kidwell, of course, but we're making her position available at the start of the year." Reine smiled. "I encourage you to apply when the job is posted. You're already familiar with some of our systems, and you get along well with the rest of the staff."

Miranda sat, speechless, for a moment. "I have to update my résumé," she said, finally.

"Do that. I know the work we've been giving you has mostly been electronic filing, but Mrs. Kidwell's job is primarily accounting. All of the candidates will have to take a computer-based accounting test."

"Yes," Miranda nodded. She was thinking of what she needed to do to apply for the job, and what it would mean if she got it.

Outside, a black Chrysler from the car service—same model, different car—pulled up to the side of the building. Reine stood, taking the shopping bag from Miranda. "Go home to your family," she said. "We'll see you on Monday."

Miranda stood, wanting to, but not sure if she should hug this woman who was so high up in the company. She opted for a handshake. "Thank you for this opportunity."

Reine shook her head slightly. "Don't thank me yet." Then, warmly, "Happy holidays, Miranda."

"Happy holidays," Miranda said, then started towards the revolving door. She stopped halfway there, and turned to say, "It was yesterday, but, Merry Christmas!"

"¡Feliz Navidad!" Reine replied.

Miranda waved goodbye as she entered the revolving door to walk to the car outside. Miss Reine waved back, then headed with Miranda's flan for the elevators to the remainder of the office party upstairs.

·

Two weeks later, Klaas Scherer's Seattle HR department posted a hiring notice for a Junior Accountant position in the San Francisco office. The maximum annual salary was listed at $63,000 plus bonuses and benefits, which was so-so for the SF Bay Area. The HR department received 223 applications worldwide, with the vast majority coming from the United States followed by Klaas Scherer's home country of Germany.

Immediately, 115 applicants were cut for being underqualified, filing an incomplete application, or having applied for the wrong position.

The remaining 108 applications were forwarded to the accounting department manager in San Francisco, who reduced the list to 40 names. The San Francisco HR manager contacted the 36 U.S. applicants to arrange for them to take the accounting test either online or at one of the company's five continental U.S. offices. The four European applicants—three German, one Dutch—were contacted by the home office in Germany. Of the 40 candidates contacted, six withdrew their applications, five did not show up for testing appointments or take the online accounting test, and eight failed the test.

The 21 test-qualified applicants were given phone interviews by the San Francisco HR and accounting department managers, who decided on four candidates to interview in-person and two to interview via teleconference (one in New York, the other in the Netherlands). The in-person/Skype interviews yielded two final candidates who were asked to submit to financial and criminal background checks.

In early February, Klaas Scherer made an offer to their top prospect, a 29-year-old, dual German/American citizen with a B.Acc., MSA, and MBA who was fluent in German, English, French, and Dutch. After a round of salary negotiations, the candidate thanked Klaas Scherer but declined the offer. She had been in contention for a position with another firm in Germany and decided to accept the more lucrative offer there.

In the second week of February, Klaas Scherer made an offer to their runner-up candidate who, despite advice to the contrary, accepted the offer the same day without negotiation.

On March 1st, Miranda commuted to San Francisco via BART as she usually did. She walked up the stairs from the Montgomery Station into the building where Klaas Scherer's offices were, and took the elevator to the 36th floor, as she had for the past 15 months. She made her way from the elevator, through reception, to the accounting department, saying hello and good morning to the staffers she had gotten to know over a year working as a temp.

This day though, she walked past the desk by the filing cabinets where she had worked as a staffing agency employee under contract to Klaas Scherer. She entered the cubicle formerly occupied by Mrs. Kidwell, and set her handbag on the office chair. Sometime in the last month, Mrs. Kidwell had come to retrieve her personal items, and the IT and HR departments had reset the computer, desk phone, and employee manuals to default. The only indication that the cubicle belonged to anyone was a carnation in a bud vase set in front of the computer monitor.

A small note, taped to the front of the vase read, "Welcome, Miranda."

Financial District decorations

STAR TREK TERMS FOR
FREEWAY DRIVING

DALLAS LIKED DRIVING, even on the monotonous four-lane that was I-5. Stretching the length of the West Coast from the U.S.-Mexico border at San Ysidro to the U.S.-Canada Peace Arch border, the I in I-5 could stand for international rather than interstate.

Dallas had, on separate excursions over the years, driven the freeway's entire 1,380 miles. Today, he would spend seven or eight hours traveling 500 miles between Berkeley and San Diego, the same stretch of 5 as his inaugural road trip to Southern California. That trip had been during his first weekend at college—Dallas in his '85 Dodge Omni crapmobile with his high school-classmates-turned-college-roommates, Alan and Allen*.

The Omni, bought between his junior and senior year in high school, could have best been described as a deathtrap. The car had 190,000 miles on the odometer, bald tires, loose steering, an oil leak, squishy brakes, air conditioning that blew hot air, and the driver-side sun visor would not stay up. He had paid $50 for the car, which his brother determined to be $100 too much. "The guy should have paid you $50," Dallas' brother said. But, a car was a car, and Dallas would put $900 of maintenance into the Omni to coax 55,000 miles out of its then-unknown remaining four years of life.

Despite the questionable safety of the Omni and the doubtful wisdom of taking off on a road trip after the first week of school, Dallas, Alan, and Allen piled into the car to spend 16 hours on I-5 for 32 hours of Southern California fun. Along the way, they defined their *Star Trek* terms for freeway driving.

.

The most basic travel term in *Star Trek* is *warp speed*, and that's how they got started.

"Imagine how many times the *Enterprise* would have been destroyed if it took them this long to get to warp," Alan said.

The Omni was very slow to reach 55 miles per hour, the nationally-mandated limit when the car was built, and slower still to reach 65, the speed limit on I-5 during the trip.

"Hey, I'd be happy to break the lightspeed barrier after 15 seconds of acceleration. Humanity should be so lucky," Dallas answered.

"For the purposes of this trip," Alan clarified, "warp speed would be the speed limit, and the Klingons would have destroyed this car before we were halfway through the onramp. Plus, it was more like 20 seconds to get up to speed."

From the back seat, Allen joined in. "Federation is at peace with the Klingons now."

"Old *Star Trek*, then," said Alan. "It doesn't matter. Whatever the case, the USS Omni is slow."

"This vehicle was designed for maximum fuel efficiency at sublight speeds," Dallas explained. "And, if you don't like it, feel free to have us take your car next time."

"So," started Allen, "is 65 warp speed? Or, is whatever the speed limit is warp speed?"

The three mulled this over for a moment.

Alan answered first, "The speed limit is warp speed. If you're driving through a school zone, 25 is warp one."

"What's warp two?" Dallas asked.

"Add 10 miles-per-hour," Alan answered.

"No," Allen countered. "You shouldn't be allowed to go to warp in a school zone. 25 for warp one makes no sense."

"You realize we're making up rules based on a fictionalized universe," said Dallas.

"Yeah," Alan answered. "But, Allen's right. You can't maintain warp speed for stop-and-go city traffic. Warp drive is for interstellar travel."

"Like when you're on the freeway," said Allen.

"Like when you're on the freeway," confirmed Alan.

The I in I-5 now stood for interstellar.

Over the next ten miles, the three defined warp speed as it related to car travel. It only applied to freeway speed, and it would be whatever the speed limit was on that stretch of highway. Falling below the speed limit would be *traveling at sublight*, or *dropping out of warp*.

Faster warp speeds would be demarcated in 10 mile per hour increments. *Warp two* or *warp factor two* would be 10 miles per hour over the speed limit. *Warp three* would be 20 over. *Warp four*, 30, and so on. Allen said that warp speeds on *Star Trek* increased logarithmically, so the freeway warp scale should as well. Dallas said that would be too complicated. Alan said, "Who can figure all that out while driving?"

Other freeway *Trek* terms they came up with related to driver behavior.

Traffic knots created by cars traveling at the same speed across all lanes was a *Tholian web*. Drivers who sped up to prevent from being passed were affected by *repulsor beam*. Similarly, slower drivers who increased speed to keep up after being passed were *tractor beamed* or *tractored*.

The worst type of driver was one that blocked up the fast lane when there was any traffic on their right. If the right lane opened up, they would speed up to prevent themselves from being passed. When someone could finally get around them, these drivers would speed up even more to try and pass back, only to slow down again once they were in front.

"Asshole!" yelled Alan, after Dallas managed to get around one such driver.

"*petaQ*," said Allen. "I'm not sure if I'm pronouncing that right, but we could add it to our *Trek* driving terms."

"What's petohcgkhhh?" gargled Dallas, trying to repeat Allen's word.

"Klingon for 'bastard' or 'asshole,' " Allen explained.

"Why wouldn't we just use 'asshole,' since none of us are Klingon?" Alan said, more than asked.

Allen nodded. "Point taken."

"How about this instead?" Alan asked. He flipped his middle finger towards the car they had passed, which had finally dropped back. "The Romulan salute."

Dallas laughed. "I don't think that's accurate, but I like it."

Allen agreed. "It's the visual and meaningful opposite of the Vulcan salute. It's perfect."

It had been a fun, if ill-considered, trip.

Dallas wondered if his former roommates remembered anything about it. There were some parts of the weekend that he couldn't recall. There had been too much driving and cheap tequila—not at the same time—and not enough sleep. Dallas did remember blowing off his morning classes the Monday after they got back.

Cruising along at 85—warp 2.5 on this 70-mile-per-hour portion of I-5—Dallas would be in San Diego in about four hours. He'd meet Allen and his wife for dinner at 7:30, and ask Allen to explain the cultural and societal differences between the Vulcan and Romulan salutes.

.

*When the three became roommates, Allen had suggested that they go by the moniker Dallas and the Allens, like a band. Both Dallas and Alan dismissed the idea. Alan deemed the name "idiotic." Allen offered to change the name to Dallas and the Alans. "The Allen part's not the problem. It's that we would even have a name that's the problem," Alan explained.

INTERNET EXCHANGE POINT

BILL WAS PINNED IN A MUNI BUS WINDOW SEAT by an enormous backpack attached to a young Asian woman. He sighed—internally—and considered his situation. In five minutes the bus had moved approximately 15 feet of the three quarters of a mile he was still away from his destination, the Ferry Building where Market Street terminated at the Embarcadero. Everything downtown was jammed up—streets and sidewalks alike—because of a BART system power outage. With all four of Market Street's underground train stations pitch black, 100,000 commuters had come bubbling up to the surface from the multiple levels of San Francisco's transit warrens.

After leaving work and finding BART out of operation, Bill first boarded a Muni streetcar that, after a couple of blocks, came to a standstill. He switched to a Muni bus which advanced him, so far, one more block. If it weren't for the 30 pounds of presentation materials he was carrying—20% design proposal packets, 70% digital projector, 10% cables and cases—Bill would have walked the remaining distance to the ferry. As it was, he resigned himself to accepting the glacial pace of the bus, missing the Vallejo ferry, and hanging out at Peet's until the next boat.

The bus, like the street and sidewalks, was crowded. The press of the other commuters reminded Bill of playing rugby, except without the shouting. And, the bus group was decidedly more diverse than his college rugby team.

The other passengers were, for the most part, silent. The one person who wanted to converse, an older, African-American man in an olive drab army jacket, was having a hard time finding an audience. It wasn't the BART blackout or the day's traffic that he wanted to discuss. The man in the army jacket was airing his concerns about the government.

"You know the FBI used to just spy on important people? Martin Luther King, Jr., Bobby Kennedy, people like that." The grizzled man's comments got a pointed non-reaction from his neighbors—they would not make eye contact, concentrating instead on smartphone or e-book screens. Their white earbuds allowed them to ignore any dialogue attempts.

Bill noticed only one person who conceded army jacket man's existence. This earnest fellow, unaccustomed or unwilling to practice the metropolitan art of disengagement, looked up from his book to view the weathered man sitting across from him. He gave the wild-haired man a friendly half-smile. An acknowledgement.

Army jacket man continued: "They're spying on everybody now— everybody in the world! Anytime somebody does something on the Internet, or uses a phone, or sends a text—the government is recording all of it."

It had taken a moment, but the man in the army jacket saw that the man sitting across from him had put his book away and was listening. He lowered his voice somewhat, focusing on his one listener. "The government has hooks into the switches at every North American telco central office and IXP. They copy all the data passing through the switches to a separate, U.S. government Internet. All the world's data—200 million terabytes every day—the NSA is saving and indexing all of that in a limestone mine in Pennsylvania."

Bill was surprised. It wasn't what the man was saying, which was your sort of garden-variety conspiracy talk, it was that in the moment army jacket man was speaking to someone, his demeanor changed radically. He became calm—lucid—in an instant.

116

Army jacket man continued: "U.S. intelligence is also plugged into IXPs and COs in Europe, Asia, Africa, Australia, and South America. The data they capture overseas gets piggybacked onto North American-bound high-bandwidth traffic, then when it reaches the borders of the continent, the data is split off and—bang—straight on the government network to Pennsylvania. The separate network is called Internet Q; IQ for short."

The man in the army jacket laid out the government surveillance plan in increasing detail as the bus inched along Market Street.

.

Two hours later, Bill was finally aboard the last North Bay-bound ferry. Searching for a spot to park himself and his 30 pounds of marketing materials, he saw the fellow from the bus who had patiently listened to Man in Army Jacket v. U.S. Government Surveillance Infrastructure. The man was seated on the main passenger deck and had returned to reading his book (*The Girl Who Kicked the Hornets' Nest* by Stieg Larsson). This last ferry run of the day was more full than usual, but there were still empty spots—Bill parked his rolling luggage at the end of a row of seats. He sat down next to the man.

"Hi," Bill started. "I saw you on the bus earlier. We were stuck on Market Street for at least an hour."

The man looked up from his book. "Hello," he said, offering his hand. "Danny."

"Bill." He shook Danny's hand. "Nice to meet you, Danny."

"Likewise." Danny flipped the flap of his book's dust jacket over the open pages to mark his reading progress—he hadn't gotten very far yet. He closed the book.

"Sorry. I didn't mean to interrupt you from reading." Bill gestured to Danny's book. "I just wanted to say it was generous of you to listen to that older man on the bus."

"I wouldn't call it generous. He has a lot to say, and not a lot of people to listen." Danny paused. "I used to know him—the man on the bus. He was my high school computer science teacher—Mr. White. I don't think he remembers that, though."

·

Earvin White, born 1952 in Jackson, Mississippi, was the second of five children to Marlon and Martha White. Coming of age in the '60s, he witnessed a tumultuous period of American history, and being black in the Jim Crow South, the events of the time subconsciously imprinted on him hope and fear for the future.

By the time he was 11, Earvin had seen boycotts, sit-ins, and protest marches and the arrests of Freedom Riders filling Jackson's city and county jails. He had seen threats and violence against civil rights activists and the funeral procession for murdered NAACP leader Medgar Evers. He didn't understand the significance of the Civil Rights Act in 1964 or the Voter Rights Act in 1965, but Earvin's parents told him and his brothers and sisters that these were both good things for people of color.

In 1966, James Meredith, the first black person to enroll at the University of Mississippi, spoke at a rally in Jackson. It was at that rally that 14-year-old Earvin decided that not only would he go to college, it would be at Ole' Miss. This worried Earvin's mother—not only was college a financial stretch for the White family, she did not want her son tempting violence at a desegregated-in-name-only institution. She tried to steer her son's ambitions to Jackson State University or Tougaloo College (both local, historically black schools), then later narrowed the choice to Tougaloo after police killed two young black men during anti-war protests at Jackson State.

In 1970, with the draft in effect as Earvin was poised to turn 18, Mrs. White was anxious for her son to attend college so that he would be eligible for an educational deferment. A bright student, Earvin was on track for a scholarship to Jackson State. Instead, his girlfriend broke up with him before the senior ball, extinguishing his enthusiasm for the upcoming summer, and college, and everything.

On his 18th birthday, Earvin White walked into the U.S. Armed Forces recruitment office in Jackson and volunteered for the Army. When he told his parents, his mother cried. On the day of his high school graduation ceremony, Earvin was on a Greyhound bus to Fort Leonard Wood, Missouri, for basic training. 14 weeks later, Private 2nd Class White was sent to Cam Ranh, Vietnam as a rifle platoon RTO (radio telephone operator).

In two years of combat in Vietnam, Earvin largely forgot his high school heartache. He had marched in the jungle in the dead of night and slept on the ground in the rain. He had been under fire over a hundred times and seen dozens of his platoon members wounded or KIA'd. He had used mess kit pieces to field-repair his busted PRC 77 transceiver after it caught shrapnel from a VC mortar. His jury-rigged radio, unable to receive, still worked enough to call in a fire mission that saved the lives of Earvin and the remaining members of his pinned-down platoon.

Earvin spent his last year back in the States, at the Army's 4th Replacement Training Center at Fort Ord, Monterey, California. Promoted to sergeant, his duty at Fort Ord was overseeing basic training for conscientious objectors, young men who reported for their draft enlistment, but who vowed they would not raise arms against an enemy. Of the 12,000 men undergoing training at the base, Earvin's CO classes usually numbered less than eight recruits. He told his final group of charges, "I don't blame you for not wanting to fight. I don't even know why we're over there."

At the end of 1973, Earvin was discharged from the Army and returned to Mississippi. He found that little had changed in Jackson in three years—his family, friends, church, schools, job opportunities—all were virtually the same as when he had left. The civil rights progress of the late '50s and '60s had not yet affected much change in the racial attitudes of most Southerners.

Home was familiar, but Earvin found life in Jackson more confining than comforting. While the Army was nowhere near equal in opportunities for non-white soldiers, it was far more racially integrated than the state of Mississippi. Going back to the status quo in Jackson was going backwards. After three months, Earvin repacked his footlocker and left Jackson for the second time. He would not return again.

Earvin headed back to California. A Chicano rifleman that had rotated through Earvin's platoon used to talk about his hometown of San Jose, a city of farms and orchards where all races—white, black, brown, yellow—got along. Based on this idyllic portrait, and not the immensely popular Dionne Warwick song, Earvin chose to go to San Jose.

In 1974, San Jose was not the agricultural community Earvin had imagined, nor were race relations as rosy as had been advertised, but the city still seemed like it was a century ahead of Jackson. Earvin found an apartment, and took the first two jobs he could, part-time at 7-Eleven and McDonald's.

Using the G.I. Bill, he started taking classes at San Jose City College, transferring to San Jose State University after two years. In 1978, Earvin became the second of Marlon and Martha White's children to graduate from college—his youngest sister had been the first at Jackson State. With a degree in electrical engineering, Earvin found a job at AT&T as a network engineer. He worked at AT&T through the Ma Bell breakup, but decided to change careers as the company transitioned to Pacific Bell.

Earvin went back to school to get a teaching credential, and in 1987 left PacBell for the San Jose Unified School District. He started, as most teachers do, as a substitute. After two years he secured a position teaching math at Leland High. After a few years, Earvin also started teaching computer science.

In 1997, 25 years after returning from Vietnam, Earvin visited the Golden Gate National Cemetery in San Bruno, about 40 miles north of San Jose. He found the grave marker for PFC Enrique Galvez, who had introduced himself in the fall of 1971 as "Rick." The platoon's sergeant redubbed Galvez "Ricky Ricardo" and then shortened that back down to "Ricardo," which stuck. Earvin complained to Ricardo's headstone about San Jose not being the paradise he had made it out to be and then apologized for not visiting Galvez's parents. He said that after 25 years it felt too late to look in on them—if they were even still alive or in San Jose. Whatever the case, Earvin said he didn't know what he would say.

"I was going to give this to your folks," Earvin told Ricardo's grave, "I'll leave this for you here because you complained so much about the Army never giving you yours even though you had qualified for it." He left a small medal, an iron cross with a three-ring bullseye in the center with an attached banner reading "RIFLE," on top of the grave marker. Earvin left, and having said his peace, felt some relief from the guilt he had been carrying for a quarter-century.

Six days later, on Memorial Day, Enrique's sister visited her brother's grave. She found the rifle sharpshooter medal there, but did not know who had left it or why. She took it home to keep with the flag that had covered her brother's casket during his funeral.

In 1999, Earvin traveled to the Vietnam Veterans Memorial in Washington, D.C., to see the memorial wall and find the names of men he had served with who hadn't made it back. He visited the Lincoln Memorial and sat on the steps where Martin Luther King, Jr. gave his "I have a dream" speech. Tourists walked around the memorial, taking their photos with the seated Abraham Lincoln and looking out over the reflecting pool to the Washington Monument.

In 2006, concerned with progressive lapses in his short-term memory and recurring episodes of confusion, Earvin asked his doctor for a neurological check up. After several visits and cognitive tests he was diagnosed with early onset Alzheimer's disease. In the summer of 2007, Earvin, or Mr. White as most of the faculty, staff, and students at Leland High had known him, quietly retired from teaching. Outside of his doctor's office, only the principal at the school and the HR administrator at the school district, who was putting through his disability claim, knew about Earvin's worsening condition. Leaving without fanfare, he told his coworkers that he had saved up enough to go traveling around the U.S. and that he wanted to visit all of the national parks.

When Leland High School started again in fall 2007, many of Mr. White's returning homeroom, math, and computer science students were surprised to find he had retired. Two of his AP Calculus seniors circulated a "Congratulations Mr. White" poster to sign and send to their departed instructor. The poster had over a dozen messages on it before it had to be scrapped and restarted because of unfortunate statements written by one disrespectful student. In the end, over 50 sophomores, juniors, and seniors signed their well-wishes, admiration, and jokes on the poster-sized card. If the 4,700+ students Earvin had worked with in 20 years of teaching had also had the opportunity, many hundreds of them would have congratulated him as well.

Leland High's principal brought the card to Mr. White's new address. Earvin had moved from his tiny one-bedroom apartment—the one he had taken when he first came to San Jose—to a tiered-care retirement community. Earvin knew that, at some point, his mental faculties wouldn't be up to the task of navigating modern-day life. When that day came, he would be moved from his independent living quarters to a room on one of the assisted living floors. In the final stages of his condition, he would be moved up to hospice care on the sixth floor.

Explaining the situation to his former principal, Earvin said that the view would be better, but he wouldn't know it. The principal remarked that it seemed like the facility was preparing its residents for Heaven by moving them up one floor at a time. "Nothing wrong with that," Mr. White agreed.

Before he left, the principal brought out the card Mr. White's students had made. It brought a smile to Earvin's face. He read the card later, after the principal had gone. Some of the messages made him smile, a few left him shaking his head. A particularly bad math joke made him laugh out loud.

In the next year-and-a-half, Earvin visited six national parks: Grand Teton, Joshua Tree, Olympic, Zion, Yellowstone, and Yosemite. He sent postcards back to the principal at Leland High who shared them on the staff bulletin board.

By 2009, Earvin was still living independently, but no longer had the confidence to take a long trip on his own. In 2010, at age 58, Earvin was being more closely monitored and staff at the care facility were considering when to move him to a managed floor. A neuropsychologist would make that determination.

·

Danny continued. "He's different now. Some form of dementia, it appears."

"I'm sorry to hear that," said Bill.

"It seems like he's being cared for. Before I got off the bus I asked him if he knew where he lived," Danny said. "The address he gave me is for a managed care residence in Colma."

"It seems like you know about this type of situation."

"A bit."

"In any case, sorry again for interrupting you." Bill fished a business card out of his shirt pocket and handed it to Danny. "This is me."

Danny produced a card of his own. "For your collection." He handed it to Bill.

Bill looked at the card. It was simple; a matte white, thick card with a slight texture. On the front it had one line of centered type: DANIEL SAAPULOA. On the back was an email address, also centered.

Danny returned to reading his book. Bill crossed his arms and closed his eyes. When the ferry docked in Vallejo an hour later, the two men parted ways with a nod.

Bill's ride, Art, was waiting for him in the parking lot. He helped Bill stow the projector and other bags in the trunk of the car.

"Sorry for the delay," Bill said.

"Not a problem," said Art. "Hell of a commute for you today."

Bill thought for a moment before responding. "It was interesting. Long, but interesting."

Where Market meets the Embarcadero

"COMB ON SIDEWALK," DIGITAL PRINT ON PHOTOGRAPHIC EMULSION, 2010

ANDRES WAS LOOKING AT A PHOTO.

It was a brightly hued image of a pocket comb laying on concrete and reminded him of the picture quality on his family's old 36-inch TV when it had been on its last legs. The details on the photo were sharp, though, while the images on the old Sony Trinitron had had a smeared, motion-blur effect to go along with their super-saturated colors. When the Sony had started to go, Andres and his brothers suggested to their parents that they buy a new, flat-panel, high-definition TV. This had been a year before the digital TV transition in the U.S.—buying a non-HD, picture tube television would have been a mistake.

The four boys were able to convince their father to not buy a new 'old' TV, but he hadn't given up on his current 'old' TV. So, Andres' older brother, who, after his divorce, was once again living at home with his parents, helped his father disconnect and transport the Sony to the nearest (and one of only six) television repair shops in the city. After examination, the verdict from the electronics repairman was that he could fix the set, but that Andres' father would be better off spending the money on a new TV.

In the end, Andres' father netted $40 on the (non-)repair. Faced with the prospect of lugging the unwieldy, 240-lb. television back to his parents' house, Andres' brother asked the shop owner how much he would pay for the set as parts. Considering the original $599 cost of the

TV, depreciated 12 years from when it was state-of-the-art, 40 bucks was as good as they were going to get.

Two days later, Andres' brother brought home a 47-inch LED HDTV that he had been eyeing online for several months. Shocked by the size of it, Andres' mother told her eldest to return it—"It's too expensive. We don't need TV that much," she said.

Andres' brother told his parents to consider it a year's rent (not that they expected rent from their son). When he saw the new flat panel for the first time, Andres calculated that it was probably worth a month of San Francisco one-bedroom-apartment rent (~$2800).

Though he had grown up watching the old 36-inch, which had seemed gigantic when his father first unveiled it, Andres felt no nostalgia for it now that it was gone. He preferred everything about his parents' new HDTV over their old CRT. The digital present superseded the analog past.

The photo Andres was looking at, though, 12x12-inches, mounted at eye level in a row of other 12x12 photos in the first floor gallery at the Yerba Buena Center for the Arts, was digital mimicking analog. All of the 100 identically mounted photos, part of an exhibition titled "iPhoneography," had been shot digitally with Apple iPhones and output analog-ly onto photographic paper. Most of the images had been captured with the year-old iPhone 3GS, but several had been shot with the new iPhone 4, which had a dramatically better camera-software combination.

Despite the 4's technological advantage, Andres liked many of the 3GS photos more. "Better camera doesn't equal better photographer," he thought.

.

Andres had become a fan of the new iPhone, partly because it was a beautifully engineered piece of technology, but more recently, and perhaps more actually, because it had enabled him to spend time with his coworker Miranda, whom he had a crush on.

Miranda had never had a smartphone before, nor even really wanted one. It was the impending demise of her six-year-old LG flip phone, coupled with her being hired at Klaas Scherer, which had a subsidized smartphone benefit for its employees, that led her to purchase an iPhone 4. She placed her order through Klaas Scherer's IT department, where Andres was in charge of mobile devices.

The iPhone 4 order had led Andres to call Miranda to let her know her phone had arrived. And, today he had spent a half-hour working with her, setting up her new phone and showing her how to use it for email, calendar, web browsing, accessing work files via VPN, and calling and voicemail. Miranda said that she primarily used her old phone as 1. a clock, 2. a toll-free phone for calling her family in Fresno, and 3. a way to text message said same family in Fresno, but mostly her older, teenaged daughter, who increasingly did not want to talk on the phone to her mother. Miranda couldn't imagine spending time looking at websites, or reading email or documents on a phone screen.

"It's a very sharp screen," Andres said. "You can look at photos and even videos," he told Miranda, launching the YouTube app and playing *Evolution of Dance*, which he had cued up earlier.

"That is pretty good," Miranda conceded when the video had finished. "My daughter has a BlackBerry, but her classmates now have iPhones, so she wants one, too."

"All the kids are getting them," said Andres, not realizing Miranda considered him to be in the 'kids' category as well.

He went on to explain that the new phone had an excellent camera and showed Miranda some photos he had on his own iPhone 4. "These are wonderful," she said, "It's a shame to see them so small."

"Actually, the quality is high enough for photographic prints," said Andres. "One of my college friends has iPhone photos in an exhibition at Yerba Buena Center."

Miranda was surprised. "Really?"

"Really," Andres replied. "You know, if you like," Andres smiled as casually as he could, "we could walk there during lunch one day and I could show you." He held his breath waiting for Miranda's reaction.

Miranda nodded. "Yes, let's do that. My daughter is very interested in photography. No wonder she wants an iPhone."

.

Andres stepped back from the row of wall-mounted photographs at Yerba Buena Center. He was trying to locate his friend's two photos, the descriptions of which he had asked for via text. His friend, Cynthia, replied back quickly by messaging him the two black-and-white photos.

The first image was grainy and indistinct, divided evenly between light on the top and dark on the bottom. A line of faint, tree-like shapes stood on the horizon. Cynthia had titled it "Traveling through the early, fog-shrouded mystery."

The second image primarily featured three, thick, white stripes on what looked like asphalt. The stripes and pavement were overlaid with a long shadow and one of the stripes had tire marks running along it. "Shattuck and University," read the text message caption.

Andres located the photos mounted side-by-side on one of the other walls of the exhibit and walked over to look at them. There was something impressive about seeing the images rendered large and exhibited in an art gallery. He texted Cynthia, "Found your photos. You are a total artist."

"Too bad I spent 4 years on the CS degree," she sent back. "Could've gotten a jump on being a starving photographer instead of a starving app programmer :P"

Andres admired the details on Cynthia's photos for a moment longer. He looked forward to showing them to Miranda later in the week.

22,000 WORDS

MIRANDA, IN HER SMALL RICHMOND APARTMENT, was looking at a stranger's photos.

She was looking at prints—22 of them, mostly in color, some in black-and-white—but the photos had originally come to Miranda digitally, on a memory card inside a peppermints tin.

.

The card and tin had come "from a tree," according to the younger of her two daughters. When Miranda asked her 15-year-old girl where her youngest had found the peppermint box, the teenager clarified, "Seriously, mom, she found the thing under a tree."

The mint tin, as found, had been enveloped in layers of plastic wrap. It had, at some point, been buried at the base of a sapling in a defunct store parking lot on the outskirts of Fresno. Over the years, the tree had grown and its roots and the weather had slowly unearthed the mummified box until, one day, Miranda's little one found it.

Miranda's daughter took her discovery to *abuela*'s house, where she and her big sister were living while Mama worked in San Francisco. She unwrapped the plastic package and discovered a metal box, red and white with words on one side and plain silver on the other.

The largest word on the box was 'ALTO1DS,' a name that made no sense in English or Spanish to the then 6-year-old. She could read the words 'STRONG MINTS,' though, so she had a pretty good idea of what ALTO1DS were.

Despite what the box read, Miranda's daughter decided that what she had found was a camera like her dad's silver one that her big sister used for school. With the drawn-on addition of a lens and flash, Miranda's youngest happily began taking pictures with her mint box-turned-camera.

A little less than a year later, Miranda's now-7-year-old gave the ALTO1DS camera to Miranda. It was the little girl's Christmas present to her mother though she hadn't said so because she had only decided to do it the day after the holiday. Also, she hadn't had a ribbon to tie around it.

Miranda had been surprised to find a digital memory card encased in the peppermint box and asked her daughter about it. Her little girl, who had never opened the tin, was unfazed. "It must have been included," she told her mother.

.

Yesterday, Miranda had brought the mint tin to work to ask Andres from the IT department if he could make anything of its contents. He identified the hard plastic square labeled 'SanDisk 128MB Compact Flash®' as a digital camera memory card—low in capacity by current standards. Andres remarked that recycling the mint box with silicone rubber inserts into a memory card case was "pretty cool."

After Miranda explained that her youngest daughter had found the tin and memory card buried underneath a tree, Andres was fascinated. He offered to see what, if anything, was stored on the card. He was eager to help, and sweet, and Miranda suspected that he liked her. (She was right.)

It had taken a day, but Andres had returned to Miranda's desk this morning with the memory card, its tin, and a Walgreens photo department envelope. "I emailed the images to you," Andres said, "but I thought looking at them as prints might be easier."

Miranda opened the envelope and removed the small stack of photos. The one on top was of a ferris wheel and a saucer-shaped structure against the sky.

"They look like someone's vacation pictures," Andres said. "Lots of landmarks. This is the Space Needle in Seattle."

Miranda shuffled the Space Needle photo to the back of the stack. The next photo was in black-and-white—a huge rock formation rising out of pine trees into the mist.

"That's El Capitan in Yosemite park," Andres said.

"Let's look at all of them together," Miranda suggested. She got up and moved to the break room—Andres following—and laid the photos out neatly on a table, one at a time.

They sorted the photos into locations—Seattle, Los Angeles, Maui (probably), and Yosemite—first, by landmarks, then, by feeling. The Hawaii beach photos differed perceptibly, maybe tropically, from the Los Angeles beach photos. Similarly, downtown L.A. differed from downtown Seattle— the architecture maybe, or the quality of the light.

There was a young woman in most of the photos—early– or mid-20s, white, with light brown hair. She was posing in many of the images— smiling, or looking over her shoulder, or gesturing towards a point of interest like a game show model. Some of the photos were candids—the young woman in the distance on the beach in Hawaii; another of her drinking a milkshake through a straw at a diner.

"She's pretty," Miranda said. She thought Andres might also have thought so, but he didn't comment.

In all of her photos, save one, the young woman was by herself. In a shot with an out-of-focus Seattle skyline in the background, the young woman, eyes closed, was kissing a young man on the cheek. The man, Asian with spiky black hair, was smiling. He had seemingly taken the photo himself by holding the camera at arm's length.

"They were in love," Miranda had told Andres in the break room at work. "But it didn't last," she concluded.

"How do you know?" Andres asked.

Miranda looked at the 22 photos on the break room table. "You can see it," she said.

·

Standing at her kitchen table, Miranda separated the photo of the young couple from the others, then arranged the remaining Seattle photos after it. She sorted the L.A. photos—where the young woman seemed less close—next. Then, the pictures from Hawaii where the young woman was distant and no longer posed for the photographer.

Miranda arranged the black-and-white photos from Yosemite last. It had been winter when the images—stark and cold—had been captured. The young woman, so present in the other photos, was absent from the snow-covered scenes.

Miranda looked back at the photo of the young couple in Seattle. The two had looked so happy and in love then. She wondered what had happened between them and where the young man and young woman were now.

"I'm sorry it didn't work out," she told the couple, glancing across their story laid out on her kitchen table.

Maui (probably)

@MARGARET2247

"WHO'S MARGARET2247?" Samantha asked. "Sorry for reading over your shoulder," she added.

Dallas swiveled his office chair to face his coworker. "No big deal," he said.

On his iMac, a web browser window open to Dallas' Twitter page showed that margaret2247 had replied to his most recent post. Her reply read:

"@dalafornia I tried to like your message but retwittered it instead. My kids thought it was funny!"

Dallas' tweet which margaret2247 had attempted to 'like' was:

"Today is the first day of the rest of your week. #happymonday"

Dallas thought for a moment before returning to Samantha's question. "margaret2247 is a 50-something-year-old waitress at a Denny's off I-8 in El Cajon, California. She's divorced, likes owls and owl keepsakes, does country line dancing for exercise, and is taking a calligraphy class."

Samantha's eyebrows raised. "That's an oddly random, oddly specific bio."

"Her birthday is August 8th," Dallas continued. "She has two adult children in Arizona and Connecticut, one grandchild, a 14-year-old cat, and a three-year-old black lab."

"Okay, how much of that is made up?"

Dallas shrugged. "None of it by me, I assure you." He turned back to his computer to click on margaret2247's icon, launching a page of her Twitter posts and conversations:

"Feet are tired but still going to Rhinestones & Lace - new step tonite!"

A photo of a fat orange tabby cat sleeping in a sunny spot on a kitchen floor followed the caption "Daisy is lazy."

Further down the page, there was a short Twitter conversation between margaret2247 and two others. It started with a post from autumn_in_june:

"@margaret2247 Happy birthday, Mom! Tanya says Happy Birthday too." The message accompanied a photo of a young woman helping a toddler walk in a small front yard.

A reply from CraptainMorgan read, "@autumn_in_june @margaret2247 Happy birthday, Mom."

The last message in the thread was from margaret2247. "@autumn_in_june @CraptainMorgan Thanks, you 2! I can't wait to see you all on Thanksgiving!"

Samantha scanned the dozen posts presented on Dallas' iMac screen. She looked at margaret2247's profile pic, an overexposed headshot of a caucasian woman with chin-length brown hair. The blown-up, low-resolution pixels hid some of it, but shadows at the corners of her eyes and around her smile suggested middle-age wrinkles.

Samantha looked from the screen to Dallas. "So… why are you cyberstalking this woman? Is she your type?"

"Could be," said Dallas, turning back again towards Samantha. "I used to show up at her place in the dead of night, ask for food, and she would bring it to me. That's two-thirds of the boxes on my 'type' checklist."

"Uh-huh," said Samantha.

"When I lived in San Diego," Dallas explained, "I used to work graveyard at Kinko's. I'd get out of work at 4 a.m. and a lot of times I'd stop in at Denny's before going home. Maragret—margaret2247—was the graveyard-shift waitress.

"After getting breakfast there the first couple of times, I recognized that it was always the same waitress. She was a tired, mid-40s woman, who was always prompt and made sure her customers were taken care of."

"And, you fell in love," added Samantha.

"Not quite," Dallas said. "But, I did wonder about her. Who was she? What was her life like? She didn't wear a wedding ring—was she married? Was she happy waiting tables in the middle of the night? In the middle of her life?

"I used to wonder about the other pre-dawn regulars there, too. Local cops; sometimes the CHP—they did not get along. Construction guys with work boots and orange safety vests. Two women in businesswear and running shoes—one would always order fruit and the other would just have coffee.

"The construction guys would chat with Margaret a bit, but it was mostly generic stuff—the weather, the Chargers or the Padres. Nothing personal."

Samantha pulled up a chair from a neighboring cubicle and sat down. "If you were so curious about this woman, why didn't you just talk to her?"

"Not sure," Dallas said. "Maybe because she was just the waitress and I was just the customer. Also, I didn't really feel like talking to anyone. I just wanted a chicken-fried steak and some eggs before going home."

"I see."

"One morning I came in and Margaret wasn't there—a younger waitress was taking orders. She was terrible. I came in two more times that week and it was the same girl. 'Great,' I thought. The next week I came in and it was yet another waitress—she was better. After seeing her for two weeks in a row, I asked the new waitress what had happened to Margaret. She said that Margaret had had a health issue, but she would be returning to work in a week or two."

"She came back?"

"She did. Two weeks later I came in and Margaret was there with her left leg in a brace. She greeted me at the hostess station and led me to a table, hobbling the whole way. Before I could ask, she told me, 'I had a little accident at home, but everything's better now.' She actually did look happier than I'd ever seen her before."

"You didn't ask about her accident?"

"No, but I did ask if she should even be back at work. Her splint went from her hip all the way to her foot. She said, 'I was going crazy sitting around at home. I'd rather be limping around here.'

"Second story, less than a year later: One night I pulled into the Denny's parking lot and it was half-full. Usually there would only be three or four cars—that night there were more than a dozen. As soon as I entered the restaurant I found out who the extra cars belonged to: sorority sisters from some San Diego State sorority house. They had gone to Tijuana to party, and had come back, en masse, to have breakfast.

"The Denny's graveyard staff consisted of just one cook and just one waitress—Margaret. That night's 4:30 a.m. customers were some of the regulars—three El Cajon police officers, the two businesswear/Reebok women, and me—and maybe 40 Kappa-something-something sorority girls, half of whom were drunk."

"Nice," said Samantha, shaking her head.

"The sorority girls were loud, and were all asking for service. 'Excuse me, we're ready to order.' 'Could we have some water here, please?' I was annoyed—couldn't they figure out there was only one waitperson there?"

"Probably not."

"One of the cops got up and went around asking the girls to be patient, which quieted the crowd somewhat.

"In any case, Margaret saw me at the hostess stand. She served the eight glasses of water she was carrying on a tray to two booths of sorority girls, then showed me to a table and took my usual order. She served all of the regulars first, and somehow managed to keep the sorority house under control. I think I left her a ten-dollar tip—a lot of money for me back then.

"And, that was about six years ago. There was a fire at that Denny's and it was closed for renovation. I moved back to Northern California before the location reopened."

"The end," said Samantha. "Except—"

"Except," picked up Dallas, "when I was in San Diego last week, I saw that the Denny's off I-8 was open again."

"And you stopped in for breakfast at 5 a.m.," Samantha guessed.

"Nope. I stopped in for dinner with my friends after we had gotten out from a movie. It was around 7 p.m."

"What did you go see?"

"*Inception*, we saw it in IMAX."

"Oh, I liked that."

"Me too. Anyway, the place was pretty busy. A couple of minutes after the host seated us, the waitperson came to our table—it was Margaret.

"She looked older—is older—but less tired. Her hair was done up. She seemed happier.

"She took a look at me and said, 'Didn't you used to come in here for breakfast?' I said, 'Yup.' She asked, 'Chicken fried steak and eggs?' "

Samantha, who had stood up and was ready to go back to her desk, reiterated her earlier thought, "How did you connect with her on Twitter?"

"I wrote her a note on the back of my business card and left it with the tip. She followed me on Twitter a couple of days later."

"The end," said Samantha.

"The actual end," said Dallas.

·

San Diego Union Tribune | PUBLIC SAFETY | Suspect in hit-and-run faces more serious charges

August 14, 2006, 3:09 p.m.

EL CAJON — A man accused of running over his wife with a pick-up truck has been charged with attempted murder, the District Attorney's Office said.

48-year-old Thierry McClintock, who was arrested and charged with felony hit and run by El Cajon police, now faces upgraded charges in light of new evidence, Assistant District Attorney Marilee Hillard said.

Last Wednesday, El Cajon police and fire responded to a 911 call reporting an injured woman that had been struck by a red Chevy pickup truck. The woman, later identified as McClintock's wife, suffered severe injuries and was taken to Grossmont Hospital.

Witness descriptions of the pickup truck led police to McClintock, who was apprehended on I-8 East through Alpine by a California Highway Patrol officer. McClintock is being held on $100,000 bail.

·

San Diego Union Tribune | PUBLIC SAFETY | Bail-jumper caught after arson at local Denny's

May 3, 2007, 10:22 a.m.

EL CAJON — A man who jumped bail last year after being charged with attempted murder of his wife was caught this morning, El Cajon police officials said.

Thierry McClintock was apprehended in the parking lot of the Denny's off of Interstate 8 after a struggle with El Cajon police officers, witnesses said.

The restaurant location was where McClintock's wife worked. She was on duty at the time of McClintock's arrest.

This morning, at around 4:30 a.m., fires set at the rear of the restaurant forced staff and customers to rush out the front door into the parking lot, El Cajon fire Lt. Noe Gomez said. Among the early morning diners were three El Cajon police officers and two California Highway Patrol officers who helped the staff and other customers out of the burning building.

Witnesses say McClintock was waiting outside in the parking lot and that he began shouting unintelligibly as the woman later identified as his wife exited through the front doors of the restaurant. One of the CHP officers recognized McClintock and ordered him to lie down on the ground. McClintock did not comply and ran from the parking lot towards the freeway. Two El Cajon police officers chased and caught McClintock as he tried to climb over a fence onto I-8, police officials said.

The El Cajon Fire Department responded to the blaze and the fire was put out by 7 a.m.

49-year-old Thierry McClintock was arrested last August for allegedly attempting to kill his wife. McClintock's wife suffered severe injuries after being run over by a red pickup truck. From witness reports, El Cajon police matched the truck to McClintock, who was apprehended by CHP in Alpine. Initially charged with felony hit and run, McClintock was later charged with attempted murder. Held on a $100,000 bond pending trial, McClintock arranged the bail and then fled.

Now considered a flight risk, Thierry McClintock is being held without bail. He will likely face additional charges, the District Attorney's Office said.

The Denny's restaurant is now closed pending a detailed arson and structural safety investigation.

YOSEMITE

AFTER TWO-AND-A-HALF DAYS OF WALKING, Henry was in Yosemite.

He'd probably crossed into the park's boundaries a day ago, but without any fences or a sign proclaiming "Welcome to Yosemite National Park," it would be hard to tell when he'd transitioned from the 1.3 million acres of the Sierra National Forest to the 750,000 acres of Yosemite.

A GPS would have told Henry exactly where he was now, but he'd abandoned the eTrex along with his car a 60-hour's walk ago. Would anyone have found the car, Henry's wallet, or his cellphone by now? Was anyone looking?

Henry had followed roads until he was a couple of miles south of Madera, then he followed a dry riverbed heading northeast into the mountains. He'd driven through Madera on his way to Yosemite before. His experience with the town then had taken all of six minutes. Cutting through the farmland on the outskirts of the town, Henry estimated he'd added about five miles and a couple of hours to his journey. The end result was the same—he'd avoided encountering anyone.

As the terrain changed from farmland to forest, Henry headed straight into the woods.

He wasn't meeting any kind of schedule, so timeliness wasn't important. Henry was more concerned with calories—how many he was carrying and how many he was burning. He hadn't planned his walk consciously, but Henry was conscious of what he was doing now. Focussing on his calorie budget was easier—and more immediately essential—than thinking about where he was walking to and what he was walking from.

147

EATING AT RESTAURANTS AND
SLEEPING IN HOTELS

MIRANDA HAD NEVER BEEN TO SEATTLE BEFORE.
She had never left California before. Miranda had never been on a plane, had a takeoff or landing, or even been in an airport. She had never been subjected to a TSA screening, which was the part of the trip that had made her the most nervous. But, here she was, in Washington state, farther from her daughters than she had ever been.

.

A month ago, Alicia, who handled travel for the whole Klaas Scherer LLC San Francisco office, asked Miranda if she had a preferred airline or frequent flyer program, and if she wanted a window or aisle seat.

"I've never flown before," Miranda revealed. "What airline do you suggest?"

Alicia was surprised, and then excited, at Miranda's status as a first-time air traveler.

"Everyone is so blasé or even annoyed at having to fly," Alicia said. "But, can you imagine? Seattle is almost 700 miles away and you can fly there in, like, 90 minutes. My husband and I drove to Seattle one summer and it took us 14 hours non-stop—except for gas and bathroom breaks."

Miranda said that she had driven between Fresno and the Bay Area before, and that took about three hours. She couldn't imagine being on the road for 14 hours straight.

"I know, right?" Alicia agreed. "Putting up with the hassles of flying is totally worth it."

.

Miranda's flight arrived in Seattle at 11:58 a.m., four minutes early thanks to a tailwind, according to an announcement from the pilot. Alicia had booked Miranda on a late morning Alaska Airlines flight and had apologized in advance for the presumed cramped coach seat quarters. But, the flight ended up not being full, so Miranda had both armrests and a window seat to herself.

Alicia also forewarned Miranda with numerous travel tips and a few airline horror stories. There was a tip on packing: "Bring one outfit in your carryon." TSA screening: "Wear slip-on shoes." And, getting to the airport: "Take BART." The travel tips helped; Miranda was well-prepared and none of the mishaps she had been warned against came to pass. The airline did not lose her luggage; the TSA did not mistake her for a terrorist; she arrived at the airport well ahead of her flight. The takeoff was smooth; the flight encountered no turbulence; and, the landing was textbook soft—on touchdown, a group seated ahead of Miranda spontaneously applauded.

The trip was still exciting for Miranda, though. SFO, recently remodeled, was a shiny, modern bustle of activity. The takeoff, while smooth, was nonetheless powerful and pressed Miranda into her seat. As her plane banked north, Miranda had a view of San Francisco she had never experienced before. The city and the Bay dropped away so quickly—became so small—that it hardly seemed real. Then, the view through Miranda's window went white as the plane climbed through the cloud deck. A moment later, the coastline and ocean below were replaced by a solid carpet of clouds. Even through the finely scratched 737 window the view from 28,000 feet was spectacular.

Two hours later, Miranda was met at Sea-Tac by a young man— Pete—holding up a handwritten Klaas Scherer sign who picked her up for the 20-minute drive into Seattle. "Do you know how to get to your hotel?" he asked on the way to the company's downtown offices.

"I think so," Miranda said. "Our travel person printed me a downtown map with the office and the hotel marked on it."

Klaas Scherer's Seattle offices were in Columbia Center, "the tallest building in Washington and the second tallest on the West Coast," Pete said. From the parking garage he and Miranda took three elevators up to get to the offices on the 53rd floor. There, she checked in with the head of accounting, and spent the next four hours learning the ins and outs of the company's new financial reporting software alongside staff from the New York, Chicago, and L.A. branches.

After the half-day training session, Shelley, the Seattle accounting manager, took everyone out to dinner at Palomino, a bistro a few blocks away. "There's a Palomino in San Francisco, too," she remarked to Miranda.

"Oh, I've not eaten there," Miranda replied. Despite her new, better-paying job, she felt places like this were outside her budget.

"There's one in Westwood," Gary from Los Angeles chimed in. "Love it."

They talked a little bit about work, the new software, and the differences between the offices and the cities they were in. Miranda was surprised to find that she wasn't the newest to the company—Abby from Chicago had only been hired the month before.

"I actually applied for the job in San Francisco," Abby told Miranda. "Looks like you had the inside track."

Miranda frowned. "They did already know me, but I was not their first choice."

Abby laughed. "No hard feelings—I'm just happy to be out of Indianapolis!" She raised her wine glass to Miranda. "Here's to us—the runner-ups!"

Miranda clinked her iced tea to Abby's glass. "Cheers."

Gary, Shelley, and Greta from the New York office, raised their wine glasses and toasted as well.

Dinner was extended as the group, egged on by Gary, enjoyed dessert and more wine. Afterward, Shelley confirmed with the four out-of-towners that they knew their way to the hotel, where Pete had delivered their luggage earlier. "Take a taxi if you're not up for a walk," she advised.

The hotel, less than a ten minute's walk away, took twice as long to reach as Gary unsuccessfully recommended bar after bar for the group to duck into. He was further disappointed when they reached the hotel and no one would—initially—join him for a nightcap. Abby relented, "against all better judgement," and said good night to Greta and Miranda as she headed after Gary to the hotel bar.

.

The next morning, Miranda woke, as she always did, at 5:29, a minute before the alarm. In an unfamiliar hotel room though, she fumbled with the bedside lamp before getting it to switch on. She then had trouble getting her iPhone to stop ringing, having never used it as an alarm clock before. She got up, took a shower, and got dressed, then headed out into downtown Seattle for day 2 of financial reporting software training.

She navigated back to the Klaas Scherer offices on the reverse of the previous night's course: right on Stewart Street from the hotel lobby; across a complicated series of intersections to 5th Avenue with its elevated monorail track; then left on 5th for nine or so blocks.

The sun was up, but downtown Seattle was not quite awake at 6:30 a.m. Most of the foot and vehicle traffic at this hour involved deliveries: food, laundry, newspapers. Miranda passed the three bars Gary had pointed out the night before; the building that housed Palomino; the futuristic Seattle Public Library; a church. A short 15 minutes after leaving the hotel, she arrived at Columbia Center.

It was too early to head up to the office, so Miranda walked downhill on Columbia Street to 4th Avenue, and entered the building through the food court.

The Columbia Center food court inhabited the multi-tiered atrium in the base of the block-sized building. Tables on the bottom level surrounded a central column and fountain, and various fast-food and counter-service restaurants ringed the different levels of the space. Several of the tables were occupied by office workers—most were sitting alone, engrossed in their laptops.

Having grown up learning from her parents to scrimp and save, Miranda wasn't comfortable spending money. With her new job, however, Miranda allowed herself to celebrate with one luxury: going out for coffee. It was a weekday ritual she now shared with her co-workers at the San Francisco office—one she had avoided with the same group of people when she was a temp.

She wasn't with her San Francisco officemates now, but Miranda decided to treat herself to going out for coffee anyway. She walked from the atrium into Starbucks, crossing under the lit green lettering of the company's name onto the dark brown tiles delineating the café as separate from the food court. Pete had mentioned the day before that this Starbucks was the first coffee shop owned by the owner of Starbucks—that the cafe had had a different name before he bought the Starbucks company.

Miranda approached the counter and was greeted by a young woman with a blonde pixie cut wearing the café corporation's familiar black shirt and green, logo'd apron. "Welcome to Starbucks," the smiling young woman said. "My name is Madeline, what can I get started for you?"

"A tall coffee, please," Miranda ordered. When it was ready, she took it and sat at a table with a view of the street outside. She whiled away an hour watching downtown Seattle coming to life before making her way up to Klaas Scherer's offices.

Milton Glaswell, who had passed away just shy of 80, had been the father of Murray, Bill's accountant and friend of the past 15 years. Murray had introduced Bill to his parents, Milton and Gladys, some years before at a holiday party hosted by the design firm Bill worked for.

Milton and Gladys were a cute couple, lively for a pair in their late 60's (Gladys) and early 70's (Milton). Milton, especially, loved to talk. "My parents left Poland in the '30s because they knew, one day, the Pope would be Polish. And, that might make it hard for them as Jews. There was also that thing with World War II."

Milton's parents immigrated to America with their two young sons in the early 1930s and settled in New York City's Little Poland, the Greenpoint neighborhood in Brooklyn. They changed their family name from Glaza to Glaswell, and got to work fitting into American culture.

"We were one of those immigrant families that comes to the United States with very little beyond a desire to live in safety and a willingness to work hard—and you know what?" Milton asked Bill. "We made it! My family is one of those wonderful immigrant American clichés."

Young Milton did well in grade school and high school, but never went to college, starting work right away at the Eberhard Faber pencil factory in Greenpoint. He went from packing boxes to spot-checking for quality to working in the company's accounting department. "I knew I had to get off the factory floor if I was ever going to find a wife," Milton said. (Gladys had been a junior secretary in the executive offices.) "Nice ladies working the floor there, but oy." He told Bill that he had wooed Gladys away from the factory's shipping department manager, who, at the time of the wooing, had the better job and better hair.

"I'll tell you the whole thing the next time I see you," Milton said, by way of goodbye.

·

'The next time' was ten years later. Bill chanced upon Milton and Gladys, and Murray and his new bride, Hannah, at the Mel's drive-in on Lombard.

Murray saw Bill first, and waved him over. He introduced Hannah, who Bill had heard about but hadn't met, and then reintroduced his mother and father.

Bill knew from Murray that his father, Milton, had been showing signs of Alzheimer's—but he wasn't sure how far it had progressed.

"Good evening, Mr. and Mrs. Glaswell. It's good to see you," Bill said.

Mrs. Glaswell smiled and said hello. Mr. Glaswell looked vacantly at Bill for a moment before offering his hand to shake.

Mr. Glaswell spoke slowly. "I am Milosz. Pleased to meet you."

Bill shook Mr. Glaswell's hand. "Nice to meet you, Milosz."

"Sometimes I forget things," Mr. Glaswell said. "If we have met before, I apologize."

"That's quite alright," Bill replied. "We met once, but only briefly, and quite a long time ago."

Gesturing to Murray, Mr. Glaswell said, "You know my son."

Bill nodded. "I've known Murray for about 12 years. He's always kept my books in good order."

"Ever since he was little he wanted to be Murray, but his name is actually Maurice," said Mr. Glaswell.

"Really," said Bill, giving Murray a big grin.

"My wife Gladys wanted him to have a French name," Mr. Glaswell said. He paused. "I miss her."

Bill froze.

Mrs. Glaswell touched her husband's shoulder, and without a trace of sadness, reminded him, "I'm here, dear. I'm your Gladys."

.

Once a quarter, Bill took his tax paperwork to Murray, who years ago had told him he should just use do-it-yourself tax software. "Your accounting isn't that complicated," Murray said. "You could do this yourself and save about $500 a year."

"Then who would I go to lunch with every quarter, my laptop?" asked Bill. "Plus, aren't accounting fees tax-deductible?"

Murray shook his head. "Accounting fees for individuals are deductible when they exceed two percent of the filer's adjusted gross income, and only the excess is deductible. I could raise my fees until they're three percent of your AGI, then you can have your deduction."

"I love it when you talk dirty about my taxes," Bill said. "Your turn to buy lunch."

After the encounter with Murray's family at Mel's, Bill would ask, at their quarterly lunches, how Murray's parents were faring. Over the course of two-and-a-half years, Milton's mental and physical condition steadily declined. Throughout it, Gladys took care of her husband, and Murray and his younger sister, who also lived in the Bay Area, helped when they could.

As her husband's illness progressed, Gladys never complained or considered putting Milton in a home, even when her children suggested it. When she finally relented to her daughter's wishes to go to a caregiver support group, Mrs. Glaswell found she didn't feel the same way as most of the other wives, husbands, and adult children in the group—they felt burdened and trapped by their loved one's illness. Though it was hard, Gladys wasn't oppressed by the circumstances of her and her husband's life.

At the end, Mr. Glaswell fell ill and was taken to the hospital with pneumonia. After a week's stay in intensive care, he seemingly recovered, and for part of a day was almost like himself again, joking with the hospital staff and the man he was sharing a room with. In fits and starts Milton recognized his son and daughter, which hadn't happened at all in more than two years, and Gladys, who he had not recalled as his wife in a year-and-a-half.

After visiting hours that night, sometime after the floor nurse had turned down the lights, Milton went into cardiac arrest in his sleep. The on-duty ICU doctor and nurses were unable to revive him, and Milton Glaswell, having seen his wife and two of his children one last time, passed away.

.

The Glaswell family and their friends were gathered for Milton's memorial at a funeral home in the Inner Richmond district. Milton's remaining sibling, his younger sister, had come in from New York with her husband. Milton and Gladys' oldest son had flown in from Cincinnati with his family. Murray's wife's siblings and parents were in attendance as were Murray's sister, her husband, and her in-laws. Scores of the senior and younger Glaswells' friends and business associates, built up over the family's five decades in the Bay Area, filled the seats in the chapel.

There was a murmur throughout the room as people picked out seats, expressed their condolences to the Glaswells, and/or greeted other attendees who they only ever saw at weddings and funerals.

Bill had taken a seat towards the back of the room. He observed some typical dynamics of human behavior—who wanted to be up front or who did or didn't want to sit next to whom. He could hear several hushed and not-so-hushed tracks of conversation.

"They don't have enough parking—we had to park at a pay lot."

"They say when you go into hospital at that age, you don't come back out again."

"He was a great scratch bowler."

"Why didn't they have a Jewish memorial?" "The family isn't religious." "Does that matter?"

"It must have been hard for her with him like that."

The conversation died down as a tall man in a gray suit stepped up to the lectern at the front of the chapel. He introduced himself as the funeral director and thanked everyone for their attendance. Turning to the large, easel-mounted portrait of Milton flanked by wreaths, he explained that Milton had requested his body not be displayed at his funeral. "It's not because I suffered some horrible disfigurement that the mortician couldn't correct," the funeral director quoted, "but, if anyone wants to start that as a rumor, it's fine by me."

The director went on to talk about Milton's life—his family's Polish roots, marriage to Gladys, moving to California to start a business, raising three children, and spoiling four grandchildren.

"That's a little bit about where Milton was from, and what he did," the funeral director concluded, "but it doesn't really tell you who Milton was, or about his warmth, or sense of humor."

The director introduced Milton and Gladys' daughter, Murray's younger sister, who took to the lectern. "When I was little, my dad's jokes were so funny, and when I was a teenager, his jokes were so embarrassing," she began. She talked about how over the years she had come full circle to once again loving her father's corny one-liners and long-winded stories, and told a favorite of her father's tales, one that many of the assembled had heard Milton tell numerous times. Before they were married, Milton had wanted to take Gladys on a romantic horse ride and picnic. All went well until they arrived at the picnic spot, where lunch was upstaged by an amorous pairing by the horses.

"After the horses' performance," Murray's sister said, citing her father, "I had to reassure Gladys that the horse and I had different intentions."

The memorial attendees, including Bill, laughed. Milton's daughter continued, "It makes me sad that I won't hear my father tell me another one of his stories. But, when I remember the anecdotes and terrible jokes he did tell, I'm happy. I hope you remember with joy the jokes and stories my father told us all."

Murray's sister introduced her oldest brother, who embraced her as he took the lectern. He paused for a long moment before speaking. "Thank you all for being here," he said. "My father was always a happy man. His happiness was infectious, as all of you who met him know."

Murray's older brother went on to explain that five years ago, his father started showing signs of Alzheimer's. By the time two years had passed, Milton's memories of his children and wife rarely surfaced.

"My father became a quiet man, which was so uncharacteristic of him," Murray's brother said. "The last time I saw him, two weeks ago, as he was recovering in the hospital, he was still a friendly fellow, but he didn't remember that he was my dad." Murray's brother paused, closing his eyes for a moment, and then opening them.

"I wasn't there on his final day, but he remembered my mom, and my sister and brother, and I'm glad to know that it was still my father inside there these last several years."

Murray's brother removed a folded sheet of paper from his jacket's inside breast pocket. "When my dad first realized he was having memory problems... when he suspected it was Alzheimer's, he wrote this short letter to my mom. After he was diagnosed, he gave it to me and told me to give it to my mom when his memory of her had gone."

"I asked my mother if I could share this letter with all of you, and she said, 'Go ahead.' " He unfolded the letter and spread it out in front of him on the lectern.

"My dearest Gladys,

"I'm sorry I forgot you."

Murray's brother stopped reading. He sagged, supporting himself with the lectern. He took a deep breath, straightened, and started again.

"My dearest Gladys,

"I'm sorry I forgot you.

"I'm sorry that I don't even know that I've forgotten anything, and am about as useful as a houseplant.

"I once wished to forget the struggles and arguments we had over 60 years of marriage, but I regret that. I'm worried that I made a terrible bargain, and have lost all my good memories along with the bad.

"Forgive me for abandoning you now, when we were supposed to have all our time for each other. Please remember for us both that I have and always will love you.

"Also, I bet Gary Edsey, who is also losing his memory, $60 that he would forget the bet first. Please figure out with his wife Angie which one of us won the bet, and pay or collect accordingly.

"Love,

"Milton."

It was quiet in the chapel for a moment. Some attendees were smiling, some crying. Bill sat, remembering Milton from the two occasions when he had met him.

Murray helped his brother back to his seat. The funeral director waited before taking the lectern again. He thanked everyone on the family's behalf for coming to honor Milton's memory, and said that the burial would be private, but all were welcome to attend a reception later that evening at Milton and Glady's home.

The funeral service over, the Glaswell's family and friends collected themselves and filed out of the chapel, Bill could hear the conversations start up again.

"Parking at their house is terrible, we'll probably have to park a couple of blocks away."

"I'd heard the horse story before, but when he told it to me, it had a dirty punchline."

"That was a wonderful letter."

.

Later, at the Glaswell's modest house in the Outer Sunset, Milton and Gladys' family and friends shared their condolences and reminiscences.

Murray's older brother had recovered somewhat, though he still seemed the most affected of the siblings. Murray's sister was actually able to laugh, as older family and friends recounted to her stories about her father. Murray himself was sad, Bill knew, but more concerned for his mother, who would be without her husband, her constant companion of 65 years.

Bill found Gladys and expressed his condolences again to her. He told her about the first time he had met her and her husband, at the holiday party a dozen years ago prior. She remembered the party vaguely, and said that if that is where they had met, Milton had probably talked Bill's ear off.

She seemed at peace with her husband's passing.

Bill asked Gladys about the story Milton had started telling him at the holiday party. "It was about how he courted you away from the shipping manager at the pencil factory," Bill recounted. "Can you tell me how the story went?"

"Oh he loved telling that story, but half of it was made up," Gladys said. "I was already sweet on Milton at the time. The shipping manager didn't have a chance."

DARK MATTER AND DARK ENERGY EXPLAINED

IT WAS A BEAUTIFUL DAY IN BERKELEY where Dallas sat at a patio table outside the cafe at the undergraduate library. It was a little after three and he was just getting to lunch—he tried to time his break for when the place wasn't overrun with students. On the whole, Dallas thought highly of the university's students. Many of them, from challenging socioeconomic backgrounds, were the first in their families to go to college. And, being accepted here—the top public university in the country, if not the world— was a doubly impressive feat. Dallas respected that.

The undergrads, though, were still young, with outsized enthusiasm for—and inexperience with—everything. For Dallas, prematurely old-man cranky at 29, the students' energy was infrequently inspiring and oftentimes annoying.

His coordinates in space-time on this occasion were unfortunate. Dallas' favored spot, a table and chair partially obscured by a support column at the back of the patio, was removed enough to be out of comprehensible earshot of the rest of the seating. On this day, though, someone or thing had left a sizable and unidentifiable mess on the chair. The tables and chairs all being fixed, Dallas chose his second-favorite of the patio's rectangular array of seating, the corner spot furthest from the door to the cafe. But, the adjacent table was soon occupied by three noisy freshmen. Before it became clear that they were going to chatter nonstop through their and Dallas' break, the other tables had filled up, leaving Dallas with no alternative.

The freshmen's energetic conversation bounced from TV shows they were watching to classes they were taking to politics and social justice (or injustice) to the world at large.

The young man seated nearest to Dallas was in the midst of changing topics. "I've figured it out," he said.

Seated diagonally across the table for four, the second young man answered, "What?"

"The dark stuff that's making the universe expand," the first freshman explained. "I've figured out what it is."

The third freshman, sitting across the table from the first, was finishing the last of his milk tea. "Dark matter, not stuff." He slurped his drink. "Or, is it dark energy?"

The second young man turned to the third. "I thought dark matter and dark energy were the same thing?"

The third responded, "No, they're separate. He's saying 'stuff,' so…" he turned to the first freshman, "You must mean dark matter."

The first freshman, sidetracked, asked mainly to himself, "Dark matter or dark energy?" He stared, blankly, into his memory, attempting to recall from astrophysics what was dark matter and what was dark energy. His two friends glanced at each other.

Reaching over the table between them, the third freshman shook the first out of his trance. "Hey, genius, what's your theory?"

Brought back to the conversation, the first answered, "Oh. Right." He blinked his tablemates back into focus. "The expansion of the universe is caused by…" He paused dramatically, "…alternate timelines."

The third freshman grimaced. "What?" he said. The second added, "Timelines?"

The first freshman leaned across the table. "Think about it! Something is causing the universe to expand, right? It's actually expanding faster and faster!"

The third freshman, remembering the dark matter/energy difference that was eluding his friend, said, "Dark energy is causing the acceleration of the expansion of the universe. Dark matter is the mass that's keeping galaxies from flying apart."

"Yes!" said the first freshman. "The universe is expanding at an accelerating rate. We can't determine what's causing it, so we're calling the force dark energy—"

"And, by 'we,' you mean actual scientists," interjected the second freshman.

"Of course," said the first freshman. He continued, "I think dark energy is actually all of our alternate timelines. As the timelines branch, they take up more room causing the universe to expand. As timelines branch exponentially, the expansion grows faster and faster!"

It was the second freshman's turn to make a face. "You're saying alternate realities take up space."

The first replied, "Why not? They have to go somewhere."

The second freshman did not agree. "Brilliant theory, Star Trek."

The third freshman, mulling it over out loud, said to the first, "The entire universe, in any moment, has a certain mass. You're saying anytime the timeline branches—like when someone flips a coin—another universe we can't see and with equal mass is created in our universe, and that extra mass is growing the universe at an accelerating rate."

The first freshman was excited. "Yes, that's it!"

The third freshman continued, "Sure. So your idea of all timelines occupying the same universe could explain all this mass we can't see—dark matter. Dark matter and dark energy would be the same thing."

Reaching across the table again, this time to clasp his friend on one shoulder, the third freshman said, "You're on your way to getting a Nobel Laureate campus parking space, my friend. As soon as you can prove and publish all of this, I'm sure the prize committee in Sweden will call you up to let you know you've won. I offer you pre-congratulations."

Dallas, his attention sucked into the conversation, realized he had been staring at the same page of his book for at least 10 minutes. He appreciated the leaps in thinking that the students were displaying, but decided he needed to find a different time and place to have lunch if he was ever going to get through his book.

.

In an alternate timeline, a seagull had not landed at Dallas' favorite table early that morning, and Dallas, sitting away from the three freshmen, had finished his book. It had not been particularly well-written, and he was glad to be done with it.

Outside the undergraduate library

PHOTOWALK

MIRANDA WAS OUTSIDE THE SEATTLE ART MUSEUM, looking up at *Hammering Man*.

The matte black, five-story-tall sculpture methodically raised and lowered its hammering arm several times a minute. It brought its hammer down to its other hand, which held a flat piece of something—whatever it was that *Hammering Man* was working on.

Miranda looked up at the sculpture against the low clouds and patches of blue sky above. Then, she dug in her coat pocket for the envelope of photos she had been carrying around and studying for the past several weeks.

Inside the Walgreens Photo Center envelope, 22 pictures were divided by location: Seattle; Los Angeles; Maui; Yosemite. Miranda thumbed through the Seattle images and found the one she now recognized as the towering figure before her. She studied the image, trying to place where the photographer had stood to capture the angle depicted. Then, she took a step forward and held the photo up, obscuring part of her view of *Hammering Man*. The position didn't quite match.

She stepped back and just a little to her right. Miranda held the photo aloft, then moved the print closer and further in her field of vision until the picture lined up with reality. (She had to close one eye for the two to match up perfectly.)

Some unknown number of years ago, on a day with a featureless gray sky, the photographer who had taken the original photo had stood right here. Miranda looked around, imagining the photographer, then, in this exact spot. From one of the 22 photos, Miranda knew the face of the photographer. She knew places he had been, that he had been in love, but little else.

She took out her iPhone and took a photo of *Hammering Man*, trying to time the sculpture's arm angle to the one in the print. Miranda compared her digital image to the printed photo, and decided to try one more time.

The second shot was good.

She unfolded her Downtown Seattle map and checked off a box labeled "Hammering Man" drawn at 1st Avenue and University Street — where she was standing now. There were five more unchecked boxes on the map, corresponding to the other Seattle photos from her envelope.

.

Earlier, Shelly, the Seattle office accounting manager, had curtailed the second day of software training.

"The vendor provided two days of training as part of the new software contract," Shelly told Miranda and her New York, Chicago, and Los Angeles counterparts. "But, it seems like the four of you have a good handle on things. We'll have a review with the trainer and then you can take the rest of the time to explore Seattle, if you want."

Greta, Abby, Gary, and Miranda had breezed through the two-day training schedule in the first half-day. Released early, Greta opted to rebook her flight back to New York. Gary from the L.A. office suggested the remaining three play tourist on a ferry ride to Bainbridge Island. "It's Seattle — you gotta take a ferry ride," he asserted.

Abby from Chicago was up for anything. She had also seemed to hit it off with Gary at the group dinner the night before. Miranda declined. "There are some Seattle sights I want to visit," she said.

After a half-hour software review, the four Klaas Scherer LLC out-of-towners went their separate ways. "If we don't see you at dinner," Gary said as he and Abby headed for the elevators, "look for us at the hotel bar tonight."

Miranda returned to the food court in the atrium of Columbia Center, where she found an unoccupied table by the fountain. She knew the sights she wanted to see in Seattle, but not precisely where, or what, they all were.

She went through her envelope of photos, and pulled out the six Seattle images. Miranda laid them out, in a row, on the table in front of her. She took out her downtown Seattle map, and positioned it below the six photos.

Andres, who had printed the images from the unknown photographer for Miranda, had pointed out the Space Needle in one of the photos. He also placed the photo of a smiling young woman sitting on a large bronze pig as being at Pikes Place Market.

Miranda located the Space Needle and Pikes Place Market on her map, and drew check boxes near them. She was stuck, though, on where to put the other four boxes.

In one picture, the young woman stood in front of a curved, red brick wall. She was standing on one leg, her arms and other leg stuck straight out like a starfish. She was laughing.

Another photo showed a huge concrete sculpture of a bearded giant emerging out of the ground and grabbing a car with its left hand. The young woman posed with the giant. Her disposition somehow made the enormous figure seem protective rather than menacing.

The third unidentified photo showed uneven black shapes stretching up to a gray sky. Neither Miranda nor Andres could figure out what the shapes were.

In the remaining picture, the young woman was kissing a young man, the unnamed photographer. He had taken the photo of the two of them himself by holding the camera at arm's length. From the Space

Needle and downtown buildings, Miranda could guess the direction the picture had been taken from and that it was high up on a hill. But, that was about it.

Miranda looked up from the photos and her map. It was still early, and the food court was mostly empty. Sitting several tables away was the young woman Miranda had chatted with at Starbucks that morning — Madeline.

Madeline was still wearing her black Starbucks uniform, but had left the green apron at the café. She was writing in a large wire-bound notebook and chewed the end of her pencil while she composed. She looked up for a moment, and seeing Miranda, smiled and waved. Miranda smiled and waved in return.

Madeline collected her notebook and walked over to Miranda's table. "Hello, again," she said.

"Hello," replied Miranda. She asked if Madeline was on a break.

"Yeah," said Madeline. "Our manager is a stickler for breaks. We're basically forced to take them."

"I'm on a break myself," Miranda said. She explained that her training had finished early. "Now I get to play tourist."

"Awesome!"

Miranda looked at the photos arranged on her table. "Do you have a moment?"

Madeline nodded.

"Do you recognize these places?" Miranda indicated the pictures.

Madeline looked at the table. "I actually haven't lived here that long, but I can try and help."

"I only know where these two are," Miranda said. She gestured to the Space Needle and bronze pig photos.

Madeline pointed to the pig sculpture, "The name of the pig is Rachel. She's a life-size piggy bank." She looked more closely at the photo. "Oh, I like her dress," she said of the young woman.

Madeline identified the photo of irregular shapes against a gray sky. "That's *Hammering Man*—a big sculpture in front of the Seattle Art Museum."

"Oh, thank you!" said Miranda. Finding the museum on her map, Miranda drew a check box and labeled it "Hammering Man."

Madeline looked at the picture of the woman in front of the brick wall. "I think this is the water tower at Volunteer Park." Glancing at Miranda's map she said, "It's not on your map. It's sort of here." Madeline waved her hand off to the right of the sheet of paper.

Miranda drew a box on the map's margin roughly in the direction Madeline had indicated. She labeled the box "Volunteer Park Water Tower."

"Aaaand, this is the *Fremont Troll*." Madeline pointed to the photo of the giant emerging from the ground. "It's under the Aurora Bridge here somewhere, but I'm not sure at what street."

Miranda jotted "Fremont Troll" alongside the Highway 99 Aurora Bridge on her map.

Madeline looked at the photo of the couple with their downtown Seattle backdrop. "Are these friends of yours?" she asked.

"No," Miranda said. "It's actually an odd story—I have no idea who this man or woman are."

"I've met the man before," Madeline said. "It was on a train trip with my dad about three years ago." She examined the 4x6 print more closely. "He's younger here, but it's the same person. His name is Henry."

.

Miranda watched people taking in the view of the Space Needle and the Seattle skyline. It was late afternoon, and the tall, downtown buildings in the distance reflected yellow light.

Kerry Park was a popular Seattle photo spot. A bus had just delivered 40 Asian tourists who joined the dozen or so people already taking pictures of the downtown Seattle vista, Elliot Bay, and the park's doughnut-shaped *Black Sun* sculpture.

After ten minutes, the tourists filed into their bus and departed, which seemed a shame since sundown was less than 40 minutes off. "They're probably going to have dinner and catch the sunset at the Space Needle," Miranda overheard someone say.

There were groups of friends here, and couples, and an elderly man walking an elderly dog. A trio with backpacks full of photography gear set up tripods and cameras aimed over the bluff toward downtown. One middle-aged couple sat close together on the low wall that bound the park from the 60-foot slope down to a roadway below.

The couple faced away from the cityscape and into the park, almost directly at Miranda. The man was trying, unsuccessfully, to use his smartphone to take a photo of himself and his companion with downtown Seattle in the background. The man turned the phone around, to review the picture he had taken. The woman looked at the photo. They both laughed. "Use the front camera," the woman implored.

Miranda watched the couple make another attempt at a self-portrait. She pictured Henry here with the pretty young woman from his photos. They were not laughing in their photo as this couple was now, but they had seemed happy.

The man with the smartphone caught Miranda's eye and walked over to her. "Would you take a photo of my wife and I?" he asked.

"Oh, yes," Miranda answered.

"Do you know how to use the iPhone camera?"

"I have the same phone."

"Great!" said the man. He trotted back to join his wife.

Miranda took several pictures of the couple, who adopted more serious expressions now that a stranger was taking their photo.

"Smile more!" Miranda directed.

She returned the phone to the man, who swiped through the images captured.

"These are great," he said. "Thank you very much."

"Thanks so much," the woman added.

"You're welcome," Miranda said.

The couple walked off, hand-in-hand, to find a bench to sit and watch the sunset.

Miranda looked out from the spot where the couple had posed. Henry and the young woman had taken their photo here too, on some cloudy day before.

Madeline had identified the view in the photo, which led Miranda to add a "Kerry Park" check box to her map. Madeline had also remembered the photographer, Henry, as a nice man, but a little bit sad. He had been traveling alone, as far as Madeline could recall.

Miranda showed Madeline the rest of the pictures from the Walgreens envelope. She explained how the images, buried on a digital memory card beneath a tree in Fresno, had found their way to her in San Francisco. The images had led Miranda to this spot where the couple just now and Henry and the young lady before had posed for their photos.

She took out her phone and snapped a picture of the view. In Miranda's photo, the Space Needle rose up behind tall, green-leafed trees with downtown Seattle in the background. The late afternoon light was changing from yellow to orange.

Miranda thought for a moment, then turned to face into the park. She held her phone out in front of herself, took a self-portrait, and reviewed it. Satisfied, she put away her phone, then took out her map and crossed out the box labeled "Kerry Park."

SOCIAL LUBRICANT

BEING THE FIRST GATHERING OF THE SUMMER, the university's unfortunately-acronymed Social Media and Realtime Marketing users group had picked a venue with outdoor seating for their bi-monthly happy hour. And, being a Bay Area summer, everyone was wearing long sleeves or jackets since #karlthefog's a.m. appearance had yet to burn off.

Conversations started out casually enough—"Haven't seen you in a while!"—as the early birds arrived and pushed together tables to accommodate the group. More members drifted in, a quorum was eventually reached, and introductions went around the tables. Folks, in turn, discussed projects they were working on and challenges—technical, bureaucratic, political—they were encountering.

After 40 minutes and several drinks, the 'formal' meeting gave way to a jumble of conversations. At the geographical nexus of these exchanges sat Dallas, who, mostly silent until now, was just hitting the sweet spot of his drinks-to-conversation curve. One drink earlier, he had been too inhibited to engage. One drink later, he would begin to ramble. For now, for the duration of his third beer, Dallas would be a well-oiled quote machine.

To a discussion on his left about developing expert skills in a field where technologies bloomed and died in the span of a few years, Dallas added, "You don't have to learn to do things well—you just have to learn to do things now."

To the woman across the table, who wished that her sculptor boyfriend would have as much enthusiasm for his art as he did for her bedroom, Dallas advised, "There's a not-so-subtle difference between passion and lust."

And, to the discourse on his right regarding the group's lukewarm reception to the public relations firm recently contracted by the university, Dallas said, "Their problem is that we're all so easily unimpressed."

With the arrival of his fourth beer, Dallas' reign as dispenser of discerning comments came to an end. Thankfully, the group closed out its tab and adjourned the meeting before things got embarrassing. The group members made their goodbyes and scheduled to reconvene in two month's time, when Dallas would once again have his brief time to shine.

#karlthefog

THE BEST CAMERA

ANDRES TOOK DIGITAL TECHNOLOGY FOR GRANTED — he knew this as he looked at his smartphone.

His iPhone 4, which had only been on the market for a few months, had 32 gigs of storage which Andres had filled with a few work apps, a few games, a ton of music, and thousands of photos.

He carried in his pocket — every day — more computing power and information access than existed when his parents were his age. In the same device, he stored more music than his brothers had ever owned, and more photography than his family could have ever afforded film and processing for. All of these things fit inside a device which weighed less than five ounces.

Andres looked around at the people he was with. There were about 250 here, gathered at Moscone West in San Francisco for the "world's first mobile photography congress," as the conference brochure had billed it. Every attendee here used smartphones to capture, edit, and broadcast photography out into the world. Andres wondered how many realized how incredible it was that they could do all these things via phones and the Internet.

Many of the conference goers were milling around in the lobby now, taking advantage of a break after the morning sessions — "The Mobile Phone Camera Revolution" and "The Shot Seen Around the World." Andres' friend, Cynthia, who would take part in a panel titled "iPhoneography is the New Debate," had encouraged him to attend the conference.

"Yo!" Cynthia called, spotting Andres among the attendees.

Andres smiled and greeted Cynthia with a nod as she approached. "How are you?" he asked.

"Not bad." Cynthia opened her arms wide as she reached Andres—he gave her a hug. "Getting mentally prepared for the panel this afternoon," she said.

"I liked your photos at the Yerba Buena exhibit. Who knew you were a photographer?"

Cynthia batted her eyelashes comically. "I do it all for you—my public. Was your coworker impressed that you know a…" she paused to recall the term they were using at the conference, "…mobile digital art photographer? Or, is that mobile photography digital artist?"

Andres shrugged. "She was actually impressed with a lot of the photos—yours included. She couldn't believe the images were captured on iPhones."

Smartphones were becoming people's camera of choice. "The best camera is the one you have with you," a photojournalist once said. And the cameras people had with them, increasingly, were smartphones.

Cynthia's panel would discuss iPhones as cameras vs. compact digital cameras and digital SLRs. The old and presumably settled photography debate had been film vs. digital. The precipitous decline of the film camera industry indicated that consumers had made their choice on the matter.

"So, what are you working on at that startup?" Andres asked. "If you can talk about it."

Cynthia stuck out her lower lip as she thought for a moment. "I can talk about it generally," she said. "Let me put it this way—what is the most used camera on Flickr right now?"

"Some kind of digital SLR," ventured Andres.

"Right," confirmed Cynthia. "But the second most used cameras are iPhones. The iPhone 4 isn't even six months old, and it's rocketing up Flickr's charts."

"Sure," Andres replied.

"Flickr was designed for desktops. It sucks on mobile." Cynthia smiled. "That's about all I can say about what our startup is working on."

Andres and Cynthia parted ways as the break ended and the conference sessions resumed. After the next two talks there was a break for lunch. He and Cynthia hadn't made plans, so Andres headed out by himself to the food court in the Metreon building across the street. He saw a number of conference attendees in Metreon using their smartphones to photograph the space, their food, and each other, as they had been doing throughout the event.

After lunch, the conference resumed with Cynthia's panel. It was well received, and the majority of the mobile-friendly audience agreed that smartphone cameras would keep getting better and eventually obviate the need for a compact camera category.

The final talk of the day was from a freelance photojournalist who used iPhones on assignments in Afghanistan and Iraq. The journo explained that people were less "on guard" when he would shoot with a phone versus his "big camera." The iPhone was also much lighter and more resistant to dirt and sand than his $5,000 Nikon D3S. Objectively, his Nikon captured better images than his smartphone, but there was a gritty aesthetic to the lower resolution photos from his iPhone 3GS that worked for his reporting as a war correspondent.

"If I were taking wedding pictures with my smartphone, the bride and groom would probably kill me," he said. "But in a conflict zone, there are definite benefits to using a phone as a primary camera."

.

As the organizers closed out the conference and the attendees began to make their way out of the convention center, Cynthia found Andres and asked if he wanted to join her and her coworkers for dinner. Andres said, "Sure," and 40 minutes and a Muni ride later, he and Cynthia met her startup partners at a taqueria in the Mission.

Cynthia introduced Trang, the project's lead programmer, and Zack, their marketing and business manager.

The taqueria was busy and crowded. The place stayed open late, had pretty good food, and was a half-block away from the small office space Cynthia and her business partners were leasing.

"The place we're renting is actually an old storefront," Zack explained. "People are always knocking on the door thinking we do computer training or something."

The foursome talked about startup life vs. corporate life. Andres bemoaned that he had a bachelors in computer programming, but all he did now was IT troubleshooting. Trang, who was quite a bit older than the rest of the group, explained that he used to do IT as a federal employee. He'd worked long enough to retire and draw a pension. It gave him the latitude at age 50 to do what he was doing now with Cynthia and Zack— trying to succeed in the marketplace with a product of his own.

"Trang helped me with those files you sent over," Cynthia said through a mouthful of taco.

Andres nodded his appreciation in Trang's direction. "Thanks for helping decipher those. I'd never seen that file extension before."

"I'd never heard of a .lee file either," Trang agreed. "Google didn't turn anything up when I looked for it."

Andres finished his bite of burrito. "I was so happy when I was able to rebuild the I/O on the card—"

"What was wrong with it?" Cynthia asked.

"Corroded contacts. Then, when I was able to access the files I was stumped."

"It's a weird format," Trang said. "When I unpacked the files and saw JPEG preview headers, I figured it was some kind of graphics format with a low-res preview, but the data left over after the preview was way less. What kind of graphics file has a preview image that takes up more space than the actual file?"

Cynthia frowned. "A compressed file?"

Trang shook his head. "The previews took up way more room than the rest of the data. Way more. The JPEG previews had 500 times more information than the actual file data."

The group went silent, searching for the answer to the .lee format mystery.

Zack spoke up. "I'm in love with the girl at the counter."

"You're in love with her boobs," Cynthia said.

Trang laughed. "Zack, her brothers here will kill you. Then, after your funeral, Cynthia and I would no longer be welcome at the taqueria, which would be sad."

"It might be worth it," Zack mused.

Two months later, on October 6th, Instagram launched as a free app for the Apple iPhone. By December, Instagram had over a million active users.

Cynthia, Trang, and Zack were stunned. Their photo editing and sharing service, which they had planned to launch in November, was a direct competitor to Instagram—and Instagram was better. They were forced to rethink their business strategy—pivot, in tech industry parlance—and see what was transferrable from the 18 months of work they had put into their project.

LEARNING TO FISH

FISHING WAS HARDER THAN IT LOOKED.

Rather, fishing for sustenance was harder than it looked. The times Henry had gone fishing as a kid with no pressure to catch anything had always been pretty easy. Henry's father, mother, and uncles used to take him and his cousins to the piers to go night crabbing. While the rest of the family would bait and set crab traps, Henry would, unsuccessfully, use a rod and reel to fish. He did once bring up a crab, but it promptly let go of the line when Henry tried to reel it in.

Henry's family used chicken wings to bait the traps, which seemed like a waste to him—he preferred Buffalo wings to boiled crab. Henry wondered now what the calorie conversion was of chicken to shellfish. Why didn't his folks just buy crab at the store?

"Catch anything?" a voice behind him said.

Henry turned to see a middle-aged African-American man standing on a nearby boulder. (The river shore here was a jumble of various-sized granite pieces ranging from pebbles to Volkswagen Beetles.) The man wore corduroy pants, a plaid shirt, and a floppy boonie hat. He also had a large, faded backpack and a worn hiking stick.

Henry cleared his throat before answering, but his voice was still hoarse from days of disuse. "No, not really," he said.

"Well," the man started, "you won't catch much here this time of year. It's harder than it looks."

"It is," Henry agreed. "I had this hook and line as part of some survival gear. I wanted to try them out."

The man looked at Henry, who had had exactly one actual meal— cold fried chicken and whole wheat bread—in the past seven days.

Previously trim, Henry had lost 12 pounds in a week—though he didn't know it—and appeared starved. He also looked haggard, having ignored his appearance since he had walked out of the office ten days ago.

"Hopefully you've got more to survive on than that fishing line," the man said.

Henry considered the box of cardboard-tasting fruit and nut bars he'd been subsisting on for the past five days. He'd started out with 15 and was now down to two. He'd eaten two yesterday and marveled at how delicious they had become over time. If hunger was the best spice, starvation was MSG.

He smiled at the stranger. "I've got some fruit and nut bars to keep me going until the fish start biting." Henry turned his attention back to the rushing stream. He hoped the man would leave soon.

The man did not. He watched Henry for a moment before calling out to him again. "Tell you what," the stranger said, "Take a break and have lunch with me. I'll give you some tips on fishing."

Henry considered the offer. He'd been fishing in a sort of daze for two hours with zero results. As much as he wanted to be left alone, the lure of fishing knowledge was too good to pass up. Plus, what did the man say about lunch?

"I guess… I could use some pointers," Henry said.

The man stepped to the ground from his granite boulder. He walked over to the rock Henry had perched on and extended his hand to help Henry down. "Earvin," the man introduced himself. "Pleased to meet you."

Henry wound up his fishing line, carefully avoiding the hook. He accepted Earvin's help down from the rock. "Henry," he said. "Pleased to meet you, too."

Earvin walked a short distance to a fallen log shaded from the mid-morning sun. He sat down and Henry joined him.

"First rule of fishing," Earvin said while handing Henry a fat Ziploc bag with a wax paper-wrapped bundle inside, "Bring a sandwich."

Henry took the Ziploc. "Rule 1: Sandwich." He nodded to Earvin. "Thank you very much."

The two men sat on their log somewhere north of the southern border of Yosemite. They sat in silence eating the BLTs that Earvin had made earlier that morning.

Henry forced himself to not wolf down the sandwich. Had bacon always tasted this astonishingly good? Or, mayo? Or, tomatoes or white bread?

Earvin held out another bagged sandwich. Henry shook his head 'no.'

Earvin continued to hold the sandwich out towards Henry. "Take it," he said. "You can pay me back later."

Henry humbly accepted the sandwich. Earvin asked him, "How long have you been out here?"

"It's been…" Henry had to think for a moment. "…five days."

Earvin said, "You looked hungry. And, you don't seem to be used to living outdoors."

Henry nodded to himself. "I've done some camping, but not like this." He looked off into the distance. "Just trying something new."

Henry unwrapped and started on the second sandwich. He hoped he was eating at a normal pace.

.

After they finished eating, Earvin said that the second rule of fishing was "fish where the fish are," and asked Henry if he was up for a hike. Henry answered "sure," so Earvin led them upriver to a trail heading east.

They walked the trail for about three hours, covering eight miles in and out of tree cover, along and across the river (four times), over earth, leaves, pine needles, gravel, rocks, and boulders. The trail rose and fell, but steadily crept upwards. By the time Earvin told Henry they had reached their destination—"This is where the fish are"—they had climbed about 3,000 feet.

'Where the fish are' was a lake. Earvin asked to see Henry's survival fishing gear: 20 feet of monofilament line, a hook, and a split shot sinker. "This is about as basic as it gets," Earvin said. "But, we can make it work."

The first thing they needed was a stick about six inches long, which Henry found. Earvin had Henry tie one end of the line to the middle of the stick—like a kite string handle—and then told him to undo the hook from the line.

Earvin retied the hook to the monofilament with a cinch knot, explaining to Henry that a cinch knot would be less likely to break at the hook if a big fish did take the bait. He undid the knot and had Henry retie the hook with a cinch knot. Then he told Henry to untie and retie the hook two more times.

Next was the split shot sinker. Earvin showed Henry how to use the Pac-man-like metal ball; pinching it on to and off of the line several times. "Place the sinker about 20 inches down the line from the hook," Earvin instructed.

Earvin produced a piece of bread crust from his pocket. "Last but not least," he said, "another reason to bring a sandwich when fishing." He impaled the crust on the hook and handed the rig to Henry—one hand for the hook and one hand for the stick.

"Throw the hook and sinker to where you think the fish are," Earvin advised. "Wait a bit, then pull the line in a little and wind it onto the stick. Repeat until you've caught a fish, or you've pulled back all the line."

Henry looked at the hook and line in his hands; he imagined himself going through the steps Earvin had told him. "How will I know if I've caught a fish?" he asked.

"If you feel a little tug, then the fish is just tasting the bait," Earvin said. "If you feel the line jerk, then it's taken the hook. Yank the line in the opposite direction to set the hook, then pull the line in slowly and wind it around the stick."

It took about 20 minutes, but on his fourth cast, Henry caught a fish. It was brown and white, speckled, and about ten inches long. Henry was surprised at how hard the fish pulled for its size.

Earvin captured the fish in a makeshift net fashioned from a mesh bag as Henry pulled the catch to the shore. He showed Henry how to remove the hook, then ran one end of a nylon cord into the fish's mouth and out one of its gills. Earvin put the fish back in the water and tethered it to the shore by tying the loose ends of the cord together and looping the cord around a branch overhanging the water.

In two hours, Henry caught six more fish. Two were too small, so they were unhooked and let go. The largest of the keepers was 12 inches long and almost got away as Henry transferred it from the hook to the stringer of fish they were keeping in the water.

Earvin spared Henry the task of killing the fish but did show him two methods—breaking the necks on two and smashing the heads on the other three. Similarly, Earvin gutted and cleaned the fish, slitting their bellies and pulling out the entrails. He had Henry pitch the fish guts as far as he could back into the lake.

Earvin skewered each fish on a stick and cooked them over a campfire he had built a dozen yards from the shore. It was a very basic recipe—fire, fish, turn once, peel off the skin before eating—and to Henry it tasted really, really good.

Earvin took the uneaten chunks of fish and sealed them in a Ziploc bag. He likewise collected the fish debris they had burned in the fire—skin, bones, heads—into a another Ziploc and placed it and the leftovers in a large steel canister. He asked Henry to put his fruit and nut bars and anything like deodorant, or shampoo, or gum into the canister as well. Henry added his two fruit and nut bars.

Earvin closed the canister with its screwtop lid and placed it in his now-empty backpack. The majority of the backpack's contents, Earvin's tent and sleeping gear, had been set up about a hundred yards upwind from the fire. Earvin suspended the backpack about 20 feet off the ground with rope stretched between two trees.

"I've read about doing this to keep bears from getting your food," Henry said. "But, I've never seen anyone do it or done it myself."

"Better safe than sorry." Earvin turned to Henry, "Do you have different clothes? We'll hang our stuff up here and let the hiking and cooking smells air out overnight."

After Henry had changed and Earvin had strung everything up like so much poorly-done laundry, Earvin asked, "Up for more hiking tomorrow?"

Henry nodded.

"See you in the morning," Earvin said and retired to his tent.

Henry sat outside his tent for awhile, wondering about this man who had stopped and helped him. Earvin had told Henry that he visited Yosemite every three years—that after a week of camping and hiking he was better able to return to "the world."

Henry wondered if he would ever be ready to return to the world. Right now, it didn't feel like it.

On the way to where the fish are

RED AND WHITE

BILL WAS WAITING FOR HIS PULLED PORK SANDWICH at the cafe counter of the Jimtown Store. Located outside of Healdsburg, the Jimtown Store was somewhat off the tourist-beaten path of what constituted Wine Country.

The morning fog and chill had burned off outside, and according to his phone's weather app and the view through the Jimtown Store's front door, it was shaping up to be a beautiful day.

Three months ago, Bill hadn't known much about wine tasting, Wine Country, or, for that matter, wine. 'Red for meat, white for fish,' was the extent of what he knew—and he'd recently been told that that adage was passé.

In the past twelve weeks, though, Bill had been immersed in wine touring, wine collecting, and wine culture—and business—working on a marketing campaign for a vineyard in Calistoga.

The Julieanne Winery was a small-sized vintner that produced about 40,000 cases of well-regarded wine annually. They'd received several gold and silver medals in North American wine competitions over the past 15 years, and they'd had at least one wine in the *Wine Spectator* Top 100 in 10 of the last 12 years.

Two years ago, the winery started conducting tours on a 'by appointment' basis. The owner—the new owner, who had purchased Julieanne in 2008—had spent $3 million to update the winery's facilities including a tasting room and retail space. Bill's ad firm had been hired to revamp the brand identity for the winery and create marketing for Julieanne's new tasting room and drop-in tours.

It had been an interesting three months, and Bill had learned a lot about wine and other things.

.

Bill had spent the morning in one of the event rooms at Julieanne. He and Art, the senior creative director at Bill's agency, had laid out final mock-ups of all the work they had designed for the winery: new logo, identity system, and stationery; wine label designs (displayed flat, and on bottles); colorful wine shipping boxes, bags, and hang-tags; rack brochures, magazine ads, and wine club materials (membership card and newsletter design); and, designs for a revamped Julieanne Winery website, online store, and email stationery. It had been a ton of work to produce, and Art and his team had done an amazing job in a short amount of time.

They had laid out all the designs on a huge, antique oak dining table that was the focal point of the space. The owner of the winery, Mr. Stoffal, who introduced himself as 'Stack,' was scheduled to give his final sign-off on the work that morning. Later, the materials would be presented to the winery's entire staff. The head winemaker, marketing director, and tasting room manager, along with Mr. Stoffal, had worked with Bill's group on the designs, but the rest of Julieanne's 30 or so tasting room, retail, and winemaking staff hadn't seen anything yet.

Mr. Stoffal—or 'Mr. Stack' as Art who was uncomfortable calling clients by their first names called him—came into the room at 10 sharp. He said hello to Bill and Art, then turned to the table to take in the entire display.

"Bill—you, Art, and the rest of your folks have done a great job," Stoffal said.

"Thanks, Stack," said Bill. "We think the work really communicates your direction for Julieanne."

Mr. Stoffal moved from the identity manual and stationery to the new-label wine bottles and shipping and retail packaging. He stopped in front of the tasting room and wine club brochures and ads, and viewed the Julieanne Winery website mockup on an HDTV Art had set up to show the design.

Stoffal looked at Julieanne's new website design on the 50-inch screen—it was blown up larger than most people would ever see it. Matching the new graphic identity Art had created for the winery, the website had a clean, modern look with solid blocks of color, large photos, and sans-serif type. The main element on the homepage was a large photo that occupied three-quarters of the page 'above the fold'—what most people could see on their screen before scrolling down.

The photo was actually a slideshow—every two seconds, the image would smoothly dissolve into the next photo. The 15 pictures in the slideshow showed different aspects of Julieanne Winery: rows of vines vanishing into the hills; stacks of oak casks; grapes on the vine in the morning sun; a group on a winery tour; a wedding in the oak-encircled courtyard; happy people drinking Julieanne wine.

Mr. Stoffal watched the entire slideshow, then turned his attention to the tasting room and wine club brochures and magazine ads, looking at each one front and back.

Bill shot Art a look—("What's he looking for?").

Art frowned slightly in reply. ("I don't know.")

Thus far in their work for Julieanne, Bill had found Stoffal to be an exceptionally easy client to work with. Stack had clear ideas of the kind of winery he wanted Julieanne to be and how the wine should be marketed. He gave his input to Bill and Art, then let them do their jobs, acknowledging that they were the design experts and that's what he was paying them for. Stoffal's comments on the various iterations of the work leading up to this point had all been well-informed and helped Bill gain a better understanding of the winery business.

Stoffal had definitely noticed something with the website and brochure and ad designs. He turned to Bill—"Bill, I hate to tell you this now, but we're going to have to change some of this photography."

"That shouldn't be… too much of a problem," Bill answered. "Is that going to set us back much, Art?"

"It depends," said Art, "on whether we have better photography on hand or if we'll have to set up a shoot. What were you looking for, Mr. Stoffal?"

"Well, frankly guys, the only people in these brochures and on the web page are white," Stoffal said. "It looks like our winery's in Sweden."

"Is that right?" Bill said quickly. He stepped up to the oak table to look at the brochures and wine club newsletter. Of all the faces in the photos—the group of friends on the wine tour, the wedding party in the courtyard, the club members opening their first wine shipment—none were black, yellow, or brown.

Art was looking at the slideshow on the web page mockup. They had used the same photography for the printed and online pieces—Bill knew Art wouldn't find any non-Caucasians there either.

"Well, that's a bit embarrassing," Bill said.

"I know there were more diverse faces in the photography your marketing director sent us," said Art still looking at the website.

"It doesn't have to look like the United Nations," Stoffal said. "I just want anyone who looks at our winery to feel like it's for them."

Mr. Stoffal watched the website photo fade from one image to the next. "Let's hold off on showing the brochures, ads, and website until we've changed the photography, okay?"

.

Bill heard his name called and picked up his late lunch from the woman behind the counter. He took his sandwich and bottled Bubble-Up further into the Jimtown Store then out a side door onto the covered patio where Art was seated at a bright red picnic table.

Mr. Stoffal had signed off on the majority of the work Bill and Art had presented that morning. Ingrid, Julieanne's marketing director, would approve the brochures after the photography changes were made. The overall web site design was approved and would go to the web team to be built out. The photos on the final, 'live,' web site would also reflect the changes Stoffal had requested.

Bill sat down across from Art who was already eating.

He was chewing a mouthful of chicken salad, but Art started talking anyway. "Mr. Stack really surprised me this morning. I wouldn't have pegged him for being concerned with showing diversity."

"Me either," said Bill, considering his sandwich. He took and finished a bite. "Stoffal: white male; early 60s; with a product primarily bought, in the U.S., by Caucasians."

"Do we know that?" Art asked.

Bill patted his shirt pocket where his smartphone resided. "I looked it up earlier. We're 66% of the U.S. population and we drink 84% of the wine."

"Here's to us." Art raised his glass bottled water.

Bill raised his Bubble-Up. "To the white wine drinkers who disproportionately drink the most white wine. And, red. And, presumably, rosé. Cheers." Bill clinked his bottle to Art's.

Bill finished another bite of his sandwich. "When Stoffal was signing off on the designs I asked him if he was concerned with changing population—Hispanics becoming the majority minority by 2060, etc. I didn't think it would affect Julieanne's luxury and wine collector customer for another 75 years. You know, as the Hispanic population grows in affluence."

"You'd think the luxury wine segment would be even more white," Art conjectured.

"Not sure," Bill said. "But, probably. I asked Stoffal if we shouldn't be concerned with the complexion of the marketing negatively affecting Julieanne's core customer."

Art laughed. "I give that a nine on the marketspeak meter. What did Mr. Stoffal say?"

"He said, 'Bill, if somebody doesn't want to buy wine because they see a brown face on the brochures, then I don't want them as a customer.' "

Art nodded his head. "Good for you, Mr. Stack."

.

Two weeks later, when the brochures and website were completed, reactions from the Julieanne staff ranged from uninterested to enthusiastic.

Coworkers who had balked at the new logo and packaging as "too modern" had gotten used to it and staffers who liked the designs were excited to see it extended in print and online.

The multiethnic-but-not-United-Nations photography didn't even register for many of the staff.

The younger, mostly white retail staff didn't even notice. One of the older, more-experienced-in-the-wine-industry tasting room pourers found the photography choices "interesting."

The vineyard and winemaking staff, composed mainly of Latinos, were pleased to see people bearing a passing resemblance to themselves enjoying wine instead of laboring over it.

Lita, the sole African-American in the retail group—and the company—was encouraged at seeing minorities in Julieanne's advertising.

She considered inviting, for the first time, her brother and his wife to come visit her at work.

One wine industry watcher also noticed Julieanne's new branding and marketing. They pointed to the new 'multicultural' advertising as an example of a small winery aware of the larger industry trend of chasing the growing Latino wine consumer market. But, they had misinterpreted Julieanne Winery's owner's intent.

'Stack' Stoffal, born and raised in Iowa, had always been interested in other countries and cultures. His edits to the brochures and website had nothing to do with trying to grow sales in the 'Latino market segment.' The round of photos he had rejected reminded him of the homogeneity of rural Iowa and the reasons he had left home in the first place.

Stoffal simply saw the world—including the luxury and collector wine market world—as more interesting with different faces in it.

ORPHAN TABLE

"I'M THINKING OF CREATING A MOBILE APP CALLED ORPHAN TABLE," Cynthia IM'd. The message popped up in a small window on Andres' laptop screen.

Andres read the message, thought for a moment, then messaged back. "Okay, I give up. What would Orphan Table do?"

Cynthia issued a series of short replies. "It's location-based." "You use it in restaurants." "You're sitting alone." Then, she explained, "If there are other Orphan Table users at the same restaurant who are logged in as 'orphaned,' the app alerts you and invites the two of you to sit together."

"Sounds like a dating app," Andres sent back. "Maybe Table for Two would be a better name."

"I think you're missing an important branding point," Cynthia wrote. She continued, "Orphan Table sums up the hopelessness that the single diner feels when they go out to eat alone. Table for Two sounds like something for women."

Andres laughed to himself. "Unless something has changed, YOU are a woman."

There was a pause before Cynthia wrote back. "A woman who watches *Sex in the City*, then."

"Just to be accurate," Andres sent, "the show is *Sex AND the City*."

Several minutes passed without a response from Cynthia. Andres wondered if his correction had ticked her off. Cynthia's reply did come, though, led by a photo.

The photo was of a man sitting behind a laptop. He was seated alone at a table in an otherwise empty cafe. Cynthia followed with, "See? This guy and I are the only two people at this place. Orphan Table could have put the two of us together so that we wouldn't be the sad single people sitting apart at an empty cafe."

Andres studied the man in the photo and wrote, "He doesn't look sad. He looks like he's working." Cynthia's IM status indicator was green, but her status message was "Working, F* off." Anyone who was seriously working would have disabled messaging. "Shouldn't you be coding right now? At your second office?" he asked.

After half-a-minute, Cynthia messaged, "Zack and Trang are being tense."

Cynthia & Co., which is how Andres thought of Cynthia, Zack, and Trang, had foundered as a group after their startup's business plan had been devastated by the launch of Instagram.

Zack had bounced back immediately, pitching several ideas to Cynthia and Trang about how they could repackage the work they had done into a different service, or sell what they had created to an established company, or join forces with another startup, or something.

Trang took a day to absorb that he, Cynthia, and Zack had been in competition with a then-unknown Instagram—and every other company or individual working on photography-based social media—and lost before they could even come to market. He wanted to step back and assess how they should proceed. He even questioned what they should view as success for their company.

Cynthia's publicly-stated goal was to quit her day job—it's why she had devoted all her free time to her partnership with Trang and Zack. Personally, she wanted to design UI/UX that she could be proud of. In a way, Instagram upending their project—which had become feature-bloated—had been a good thing.

Cynthia elaborated on the tensions at the office. "Trang said he had an idea on how to leverage some of our work into a new app. He's been programming solo for over a week now without telling us what his idea is."

Andres pictured Trang, a 50-ish, retired GS-13 programmer analyst, coding away late at night at Cynthia & Co. headquarters on Mission Street.

Cynthia sent another message. "Zack is going nuts for something to do. I'm just hoping Trang hasn't remortgaged his house to keep us going financially. He just says, 'We're fine, we're fine.' "

Andres looked again at the photo Cynthia had sent. He knew any advice—especially social advice—would go unheeded, but he typed anyway, "If you want to meet the guy at the other table, just walk over and say hi."

"If I could just walk up to someone and ask to sit with them," Cynthia wrote, "would I have started designing a tech solution that requires the combined infrastructures of the Internet and the telecommunications industry just to do the same thing?"

"Duh," she concluded.

Andres, at his desk at work, audibly sighed.

Cynthia sent another IM. "Come have coffee with me so I'm not alone at a table like this other guy," she asked.

"Where are you?" Andres asked back.

"In Berkeley."

"I can't BART out to Berkeley for a coffee break." The ride each way would take 23 minutes. "Come into the city after I get off work and we'll go for dinner. My treat."

"Okay," she sent back. Then, a moment later, "7?"

"Sure," Andres agreed. "What do you want to eat?"

"You pay, you pick."

"I'll ping you back with where to meet." Andres signed off with, "ttyl."

Andres started thinking about where Cynthia might like to eat and what he could afford. Should he pick a place where he could make a reservation?

"Oh!" Andres realized. OpenTable, Orphan Table. Now, the name made more sense.

Where BART goes

FAIR TRADE

MIRANDA WAS AT THE FERRY BUILDING MARKETPLACE
BY HERSELF.

She was by herself in the sense that she hadn't come to the building with anyone nor was she meeting anyone there. Otherwise, there were hundreds (or thousands) of visitors in the Ferry Building: local gastrovores with cloth totes; European tourists with heavy backpacks; financial district workers on break. Miranda was one of the latter.

The Ferry Building was about a mile down Market Street from Klaas Scherer LLC's San Francisco offices. Miranda didn't often range so far on her lunch breaks, but a late-morning computer networking failure had left most of the company's staff unproductive. After 40 minutes without Web, email, or phone service—all were connected, apparently—everyone was told to take an early, two-hour lunch.

She'd already gone out for morning coffee with her coworkers, but Miranda decided to splurge on a second coffee out—this time at the Ferry Building Peet's. She took her $2 coffee order and sat at the windows facing the water and the passenger ferries that crisscrossed the Bay to Sausalito, Tiburon, Vallejo, and Oakland.

A disheveled, older woman sat down at the Bay-facing windows a seat away from Miranda. The woman had short, white hair and a ruddy complexion. Her clothes were plain; rumpled, but not dirty. She set a large, to-go Peet's cup down on the counter in front of her, then bent down to rustle through the contents of a creased Bloomingdale's shopping bag she had put on the floor between her feet. The woman found what she was looking for, straightened, and placed four single-serve French Vanilla creamers and four sugar packets next to her Peet's cup.

The woman methodically added the flavored creamers and sugars to her coffee, stirring with each added ingredient.

Over the course of 20 minutes, while Miranda ate her brownbag sandwich and watched the shoppers, tourists, and lunchers pass by outside, the woman one seat away sipped her International Delight-Peet's blend and thumbed through a dogeared issue of *Good Housekeeping*. When she had finished her coffee, the woman collected the plastic creamer cups and paper sugar packets and placed them in her empty Peet's cup. She rummaged through her worn Bloomies' shopping bag again and emerged with a plastic 99¢ Only Store bag. From the 99¢ Only bag came a pink plastic spoon and a four-pack of mixed-fruit cups. The woman removed one plastic cup from the cardboard sleeve, peeled back the cup's foil lid and ate the contents. One piece. Of fruit. At a time. She finished the first cup, spooning out and sipping the liquid at the bottom, then started on a second serving.

"Can I share my sandwich with you?" Miranda asked. She pushed the neatly cut, uneaten half of her sandwich on its paper napkin a few inches along the counter toward the woman and her fruit cups.

The woman eyed Miranda's offering—a homemade triangle of roast beef on whole wheat with cheddar, lettuce, tomato, onion, mayonnaise, and mustard. "Does it have pickles?" the woman asked back. Her voice was raspy.

"No pickles," Miranda answered. She slid the sandwich further into the counter space belonging to the empty seat.

"Okay," the woman said. She took her remaining two fruit cups out of their cardboard sleeve and put them on the counter near Miranda's sandwich.

"Thank you," said Miranda. "I'll just take one, though, okay?" Miranda reached over and picked up one of the fruit cups, then moved the sandwich and the other cup to the older woman.

The woman frowned and took her fruit cup and Miranda's sandwich. "I don't want nothing for free," she said defensively. She looked at the half-sandwich. "Thank you," she said.

"You're welcome," said Miranda. She took the fruit cup—payment for her half-sandwich—and placed it in the plastic sandwich bag still in her purse. "I'm going to save this for later," she told the woman.

.

It had taken a while, but Miranda had grown to appreciate the utility of having computer and Internet access with her everywhere she went. She used her smartphone now in ways that she had never used her family's desktop computer—even before the Windows XP machine had become woefully out-of-date.

Miranda studied the camera roll on her small iPhone screen. She didn't have that many pictures on her phone—around 70—and she had pored over each of them dozens of times. Most of the photos were of her littlest girl. Her older daughter appeared in a scant six images—three from her father, one 'selfie,' and two candids that Miranda had managed to snap without her girl noticing. Getting her eldest to send her a photo had been like pulling teeth, and the resulting stern, defiant teenager that stared up from Miranda's phone seemed like a wholly different person than the adoring little girl in the three older photos Miranda's husband had emailed.

Despite missing the wide-eyed, laughing daughter that her 16-year-old had grown up from, Miranda had chosen the disapproving selfie for her eldest's contact picture. It reminded Miranda, whenever she phoned or messaged her daughter, that her teenager was on her way to becoming a young woman.

The other photos included the 22 images salvaged from the memory card Miranda's youngest had found half-buried under a tree. Miranda looked at the photos often. She thought of the images—from

Seattle, Los Angeles, Hawaii, and Yosemite—as Henry's, though there was no proof that he had taken any of them besides the one in which he appeared and was obviously holding the camera.

Henry, who Miranda had never met, and whose name she had only recently learned by chance.

Miranda looked up from her phone. On the promenade outside the window, people sat on benches in front of black iron railings separating them from the water. On the other side of the railing, a ferry sat; docked and taking on passengers. Seagulls, hopeful, flew above and around the vessel. Miranda launched the camera app on her phone, held the device up to the glass, and captured the overcast scene—digitally freezing the moment in time.

She opened a new email and attached the photo to it. Miranda addressed the email to her teenage daughter and typed in "Just now" for the subject line.

"*Mija*,

"I am at the Ferry Building now and wish you and your sister were with me. This photo isn't as nice as the ones you showed me from your photography class, but I am trying.

"Be good and be good to your sister.

"*Te quiero*,

"Mom"

Later, Miranda would also send the photo to Madeline in Seattle, who had helped her identify the landmarks in Henry's photos and Henry himself. But, for now, she had to head back on Market Street to the office. After standing and re-donning her coat, she turned to the woman eating the last of her mixed fruit cups. Miranda put her hand on the old woman's shoulder. "Goodbye, Agatha. It was nice meeting you today."

Agatha didn't look up, but she set down her pink plastic spoon to put her hand on Miranda's. "You too, you too," she said, nodding.

At the Ferry Building Marketplace

N I H O N - M A C H I

DALLAS ARRIVED AT THE CURRY RESTAURANT FIRST, which is
not to say that he was on time. He was late, but his friends would be later.
Waiting on this particular group was something Dallas had gotten used to
years ago.

The restaurant, on a pedestrian bridge between two of the
block-sized buildings of San Francisco's Japantown, was unchanged
from Dallas' first visit in 1996. It occupied a narrow space nearly the
entire length of the enclosed, second-story walkway. Dallas had always
wondered if the shops lining the left and right sides of the bridge had been
planned, or shoehorned in as a retail afterthought. As it was, the curry
shop's quirky shape and location attracted many of the anime and manga
fans that flocked to Japantown.

Dallas first visited J-Town as an anime and manga fan when he was
a freshman in high school. A founding member of Otakus Anonymous, his
school's anime club, Dallas and his classmates did everything they could
to come to Japantown as often as they could. They bargained with their
families for rides into the city, claiming non-existent school club outing
requirements and the benefits of pan-Pacific cultural understanding. The
three club members' campaigning resulted in a visit maybe once every
month-and-a-half.

OA's roster, by junior year, had grown to eight with three of the
members having drivers licenses and two of them having cars. No longer
dependent on rides from parents or siblings, the club's frequency of visits
jumped to almost every weekend. The club's car owners would pick up
members on their way to the park-and-ride, where they'd meet up to form
a two-car caravan for the hour drive into San Francisco.

In the scores of visits the club made, they had eaten at every J-Town restaurant—except the expensive ones. The curry place, while not the cheapest, was their go-to favorite. Surveying the restaurant's current diners, Dallas could see, over a decade later, anime fans still came here. There were more now and easier to spot—a group seated in a booth down the aisle were dressed in Japanese high school tennis club uniforms. He didn't know what show it was from, but Dallas recognized cosplay when he saw it.

Cosplay—the Japanese contraction of 'costume play'—was something seen only at conventions during Dallas' mid-'90s club days. When his older brother introduced Dallas to the world of untranslated Japanese animation in the late '80s, cosplayers were strictly Japanese fans seen in Japanese magazines. Now, cosplay was the norm at any anime convention around the world. Conventions, too, were no longer a rarity. In '96, there were ten U.S. conventions focussed on anime and manga. 14 years later, there were 200 annual cons throughout the country with hundreds of thousands of attendees. At times anime felt mainstream, though Dallas knew it wasn't.

.

20 minutes after Dallas, Arlene and Ben arrived. They had texted earlier that they would be delayed—their sitter, Arlene's mother, had been late. A few minutes after Arlene and Ben, Mike and Jackson appeared, one after the other.

Reunited after more than ten years, the group quickly caught up on careers and family and the cost of living in the Bay Area. It wasn't until they had placed their orders that Otakus Anonymous reverted to the dynamic of their high school days.

After the waitress came and went, Arlene said to Mike, "I knew you were going to get katsu curry."

"I'm so glad you can still predict what I like to eat," Mike countered.

Jackson said out loud what Dallas, Ben, and Arlene were thinking, "We all knew what you were going to order. Katsu curry is the only thing you've ever ordered here."

"I've ordered other things," Mike complained.

"Nope," said Ben.

Dallas concurred. "Not here."

"See?" Arlene crossed her arms to emphasize her point.

"Huh," said Mike. His face broke out in a huge grin. "*Katsu karē ga suki desu yooooooo!*" Mike said, imitating a Japanese TV commercial the club had fallen in love with during their senior year.

Ben, who had just set down his water glass, almost did a spit take. This set the rest of the group laughing and the 10+ years since they had last gotten together disappeared.

"I haven't thought about that in forever," Ben said, wiping some water from his chin.

"Glad to serve as a memory aid," said Mike. "You know, I actually have ordered other things here—just not with you guys."

Arlene feigned shock. "You mean there's someone else?"

"Yes, it's true." Mike turned dramatically somber. "There have been others." He put his hand on his heart. "But katsu curry was always our thing—it will always be our thing."

·

After their food arrived, Dallas remarked that now, American anime fans wouldn't see things like the Japanese curry commercial during their anime viewing. "Watching online or on cable, you just see U.S. commercials. Or, no commercials if you're watching DVDs."

"No commercials on downloaded fansubs, either," Ben added.

The curry commercial had been captured in 1989 on a Betamax tape in Japan. The tape contained a two-hour block of Nippon Television programming, and shipped in a box with a week's worth of other tapes to a small video rental store in San Jose. At the store, the owner copied programs from the original tape onto series compilation tapes on VHS. When a compilation tape was full—two episodes for an hour-long show or four for a half-hour—the store owner would duplicate it and put that copy on the shelves for rent.

Mike asked, "Where did your brother get that tape with the commercial on it, anyway?"

"I don't even remember what the show was," Arlene mused, "just the commercial."

"*Patlabor*," Dallas answered. "He copied a tape that he rented from a shop in San Jose's Japantown." Dallas continued, "Remember watching shows with no subtitles and following along with typed up fan translations?"

"Yup," said Ben. "When otaku were real otaku."

"Kids today have it easy!" Mike said in grumpy-old-man voice. "With their streaming services and their professionally translated, licensed titles. When I was a boy, we had to walk uphill both ways to get our anime!"

Everyone laughed.

Of the five OA members assembled, Ben, Arlene, and Mike had kept up with anime the most. They still went to conventions and were aware of what shows were current in the U.S. and Japan. Jackson had followed anime through college, but had given it up when he started dating the woman who would become his wife and then ex-wife.

"Sorry to hear about that," Dallas told Jackson.

"It's all right," Jackson replied. "It wasn't meant to be. The last six months have been weird. It's like I had put who I was on pause for six years and now I've hit play again."

The table had become quiet. "I don't mean to bum everybody out," Jackson said. "Getting separated and divorced was the best thing for both of us."

.

The group left the curry restaurant to go to the Japanese bookstore, which had grown from one to two floors since their last club visit the summer before college. The new, lower floor was devoted entirely to anime and manga and almost half of that was English-translated. Following their old pattern, they got dessert and headed back outside to the Peace Pagoda Plaza.

Arlene cornered Dallas about keeping better in touch.

"You know, for someone who has Social Media Coordinator as a job title, you're not available on Facebook that much." She added, "You would have known about Jackson's divorce if you checked your account once in a while."

"Yeah, Facebook's not my favorite." Dallas shrugged. "I'm on Twitter," he offered.

"How am I supposed to arrange get togethers on Twitter?" Arlene demanded.

"Direct message," said Dallas. "Or, use email. Or, text. Or, call me. Anything but Facebook."

"Hey, check this out," Ben said. He showed Dallas his iPhone, holding the device so Dallas could see the screen. It showed the view in front of them. He handed his phone to Dallas.

"What am I doing?" asked Dallas. "Is it a camera app?"

"Not quite. Move the view around," Ben instructed.

Dallas held the phone out at arms length and panned around. The image on the iPhone's screen showed the plaza as he moved the phone—shoppers walking, cars driving up and down Post Street. Dallas pointed the phone at the Peace Pagoda and tilted it up. The view on the device didn't show anything out of the ordinary until the phone showed part of the sky. Dallas caught a bit of it then—a rainbow.

The rainbow arced in the sky above the Peace Pagoda on the iPhone's screen—but not in the actual sky.

"Cool," said Dallas. He moved the phone to follow the virtual rainbow on the screen. It crossed above the Peace Pagoda with the ends disappearing beyond the hills and buildings in either direction. Dallas held his hand behind the phone so that it appeared on screen—it obscured the rainbow on the phone display.

"This AR is pretty amazing," Dallas said. "The rainbow is mapped almost perfectly." Dallas shook the phone to see if he could get the virtual rainbow to display incorrectly. The image held up, adjusting with the phone's movement to properly place the rainbow in the sky behind buildings, clouds, trees, and other obstructions.

"You'll never see a rainbow like that in reality," Ben said.

Dallas looked at Ben quizzically. "Meaning?"

Ben pointed out that the rainbow viewed through the phone was almost directly above them. An actual rainbow was a refraction of light that always appeared, at some distance, perpendicular to the viewer. "You can never, from your point of view, get under a rainbow," he said.

"I see," said Dallas as he handed the phone back to Ben.

"My rainbow," said Ben, "starts at our house in Concord and ends at the Tokyo Big Sight."

"Why there?" asked Dallas.

"Comiket 2012," Ben revealed.

The iOS app, which Arlene's older brother had sent her a beta code for, would let you choose the ends of your rainbow. You could specify a location, like Paris, or a future event, like Comiket 2012, and the app would find and place the end of your rainbow there. The start of the rainbow was set wherever you had input your goal.

Ben had handed his phone to Mike who was viewing the augmented reality rainbow now. "This is neat, but what is it actually good for?"

"It's mostly a demo," Arlene said. "My brother was working on a photo sharing app that had a feature where you could paint virtual graffiti onto buildings in your photos."

She explained that the app had gotten unwieldy with the number of image editing capabilities her brother had put into it and that many of the features didn't work that well. "They ended up shelving the photo sharing app, but found an investor who was interested in the AR graffiti."

Ben continued, "The graffiti looked pretty rough in the photo app. The rainbow demo does one thing, but it does it really well."

Jackson was taking a turn with Ben's phone and the app now. "The rainbow does look real," he said. "It's like the phone lets you see into a parallel dimension."

"I can send you all download codes for the beta," Arlene offered. She turned to Dallas. "I'll send yours via email instead of Facebook."

Dallas smiled. "Appreciate it. What's the app called?" he asked.

"Rainbow," Arlene replied.

THIS LIFE AND THE NEXT

"HEY, MAN, you got a light?"

"Sorry, no," Bill said to the backpacker who was holding up a hand-rolled cigarette. "I used to roll my own, too," he added. "Thought it would help me quit."

The would-be smoker put the rollie away in his heavy plaid shirt's breast pocket. "Did it work?"

Bill shook his head. "No, I just got really good at rolling. I did end up quitting though—the wife convinced me when she got pregnant."

"Everybody's quitting, man. People want to live forever." The man hoisted up his large backpack and cinched the straps. "Peace, brother," he said to Bill as he continued along the beach in the opposite direction.

"Take it easy," said Bill.

.

Santa Monica Beach was quiet early in the morning. Surfers had yet to arrive—or, maybe it was too flat today. By mid-morning the beach would populate with walkers and joggers on the boardwalk and bodybuilders at the original Muscle Beach. As the day drew on, the shore would fill with beachgoers bringing towels and umbrellas, coolers with food and drink, and books and radios and beach toys. In the evening, couples would come to watch the sunset and groups of friends would walk the beach coming from or going to the Santa Monica Pier.

Just after sunrise, though, only true denizens of Santa Monica Beach were about—residents of $2 million+ condos that lined Appian Way and homeless who camped in bus shelters and under benches on Main Street two blocks inland. In addition, this morning, there was Bill.

Bill continued his walk south, away from the public fishing pier and the boardwalk park with its ferris wheel and carnival attractions. He passed a man wearing a lush, white terry cloth robe who was smoking a cigar and walking a small dog.

"Good morning," Bill said as he and the man approached.

The man nodded to Bill and grunted a reply. It might have been "uh-huh"—Bill wasn't sure. The guy with the hand-rolled cigarette could've gotten a light off of him, Bill thought.

Further on, Bill caught part of a conversation between a city parks workman, a woman with her belongings in a shopping cart, and a well-dressed couple—a man in RRL summer wear and a woman wearing a sporty mix of The North Face and Lululemon. The four were discussing some pending city council legislation regarding the pier. Bill wondered how long they all had known each other and whether the seeming differences in their respective incomes ever came up in conversation. If they met up again in another life, would their roles be different?

As Bill followed the walkway meandering past expensive beachside hotels, he recognized a man sitting on a low patio chair facing the beach and the ocean. The man had a to-go cup of coffee on the ground next to him along with a book, Stieg Larsson's *The Girl who Kicked the Hornet's Nest*.

"Danny?" inquired Bill as he reached the man.

Daniel Saapuloa turned to see Bill on the paved walkway between the hotel and the beach. He stood and brushed the wrinkles out of his trousers. "Nice to see you, Bill," he said. The two men shook hands.

Bill apologized for intruding on Daniel and asked what he was doing in Santa Monica. "At least this time I didn't interrupt your reading," Bill joked.

Daniel bent down to pick his book up off the sand. "I'm slowly reading it through a second time," he said. Daniel was driving down from

Northern California to visit a nephew going to school in San Diego. He had stopped to stay with friends in Santa Monica on his way down.

Bill was in town for a marketing convention at a nearby hotel. It was an annual gathering, last held at a 'business' hotel in San Mateo. "I knew it was a business hotel when I saw that the event rooms had names like 'Convene' and 'Inspire.' "

"Not exactly where you want to have your wedding reception," Daniel supposed.

Bill mimed reading from a wedding invitation. "The ceremony will take place on the Synergy terrace with a reception to follow immediately in the Collaborate ballroom."

Daniel gestured with his book toward the hotel. "I'm going to have some breakfast. If you've got time, care to join me?"

Bill thought for a moment of the pending breakfast mixer he was supposed to attend with his marketing convention colleagues — danish, coffee, mimosas, bragging, pitches, and one-upsmanship. "Breakfast sounds great," he answered. "You have to let me pay, though."

Daniel shook his head. "Breakfast is on the hotel. I know one of the owners."

.

Daniel ordered eggs Benedict, bacon, orange juice, and more coffee. Bill was gauging what he should have when Daniel advised him, "Order as if you're paying for it."

"Fair enough," said Bill. "Steak and eggs and a bloody mary," he told the waiter.

Over the course of a leisurely breakfast, the two continued the conversation they had started on the Vallejo ferry some months ago. Bill learned a little more about Daniel beyond the business card info they had exchanged at their first meeting.

Daniel was 30 and ostensibly retired. His family was originally from Guam—he'd been born there—and had moved in ones and twos over several years to California. Daniel had come before high school to live with his older brother's family. "Having to wear shoes all the time was the hardest thing," he said. "Growing up in Guam, I only ever had to wear shoes to church."

After high school, Daniel received scholarships to go to Stanford—"almost a full ride"—but didn't attend. The part-time job he had taken as a high school junior to help pay for college became a full-time opportunity. "I was doing backend coding at a small company called AuctionWeb," Daniel related.

Bill searched his memory. "Why is that name familiar?" he asked.

"About a year after I started there," Daniel explained, "the owner changed the name to eBay." After the company went public, the founders became billionaires and Daniel was an instant millionaire. After five years, he sold his fully-vested options and became a multi-multi-millionaire.

From his dot-com jackpot, Daniel purchased an old Victorian in San Francisco. He paid $2 million for the 3,800 square foot 3/2, and spent an additional million to renovate it. "I never actually lived in the house," he said. During the two-year reconstruction, Daniel traveled the world.

"I feel less guilty about you buying me breakfast now," said Bill.

Daniel laughed. "You shouldn't feel guilty at all—first, I'm not paying. Second, guilt doesn't help anything." He paused, picked up a piece of bacon, and munched on it before continuing. "While I was out running around the world celebrating myself, my niece got sick. Rather, she was diagnosed with a neurodegenerative disorder."

In the same time that Daniel was able to ride the dot-com bubble, cash out before the crash, and travel the world "living all that life had to offer," his niece's fine motor skills began to deteriorate. Less than a year after her diagnosis she couldn't walk.

She passed away before her eighth birthday.

Bill thought of his own two daughters. "I'm sorry for your family's loss," he said.

"Thank you," said Daniel.

Daniel sent money to his brother for the little girl's care, but he didn't come back to see her despite his brother's insistence and his sister-in-law's pleas. When his niece fell into a coma and then died, Daniel was on the other side of the world. "After that, I was too ashamed to go to her funeral," he told Bill.

Bill stirred the contents of his drink with its celery stick before taking a sip. "I hope you patched things up with your brother."

"My brother wasn't angry at me," Daniel said. "He just wanted me to see my niece before she was gone."

When Daniel returned, almost a year after his niece's passing, his brother asked why he'd stayed away so long. Daniel wasn't exactly sure—he'd had so much good fortune early on and his niece had barely had the chance to live. It was as if all of her life's potential had been given to him. "Your success wasn't at the expense of hers," Daniel's brother told him.

"However it works," Daniel said to Bill, "I decided then, that in the next life, I'd make sure my niece got all the luck."

.

After the breakfast dishes had been cleared away, Bill considered another bloody mary but switched to caffeine instead. He added cream and sugar to his coffee.

"You said you never lived in the house you were remodeling. What did you do with it?" Bill asked.

"I sold it," said Daniel. "After a year of avoiding my family and friends, I came back to California." On the day Daniel was at his dream home inspecting the work that had been done, a startup multi-multi-millionaire rang the doorbell.

"I love this house," the 23-year-old wearing a hoodie with "sweat equity" printed on it said. "How much is it?"

Daniel told the walk-up buyer that the house wasn't for sale.

"Everything's for sale," the young man said. "Name your price."

Bill raised his eyebrows. "How much did you sell it for?"

"Six million," Daniel answered. "Hopefully he's enjoying living there."

Bill nodded approvingly. "So where did six million move you to, if you don't mind me asking?"

"A nice three-bedroom in Woodland."

Bill was surprised. "Just one? For that much, in Woodland you could have gotten 30 nice three-bedrooms."

"Just one. Near my brother's family's place."

The rest of the proceeds from Daniel's house sale went to his oldest nephew's UC San Diego college education, a trust for his younger nephew and remaining niece, and four endowed scholarships in his departed niece's name. Properly managed, the Mia Saapuloa Memorial Scholarships would continue in perpetuity.

After selling the house and redirecting the money towards philanthropy, Daniel used his eBay fortune—a little more than $23 million—to create a foundation that issued grants funding neurodegenerative disease research. Now, he spent his time persuading the wealthy to donate to charitable causes.

"I went from feeling less guilty about free breakfast to feeling like total crap," said Bill. "You've given away your fortune to advance the cause of science, and I spend my time trying to convince people to hire me to help them sell things."

"I haven't given away all my money yet. I invested a chunk of it to pay myself about 70,000 a year. And I have my house, and I have a decent car." Daniel smiled. "If it helps ease your conscience, my foundation, which is basically me and an accountant, would happily accept pro bono work."

"The way you tell your story—you don't need any marketing help. I feel like I've just gotten a personal TED Talk."

"You haven't even gotten the full pitch," Daniel said.

"It works," Bill said. "What kind of marketing were you looking for?"

Daniel thought for a moment. "A logo? Or, branding? Some stationery, at least."

"Done," said Bill. "It's the least I can do."

MONUMENT

THE FANCHER MONUMENT, 63-feet tall and made of stone, stands at the intersection of State Route 140 and North Aboleda Road in Tuttle, California. The memorial honors George Fancher, a wealthy local farmer and banker, and was erected after his death as a stipulation of his will. An inscription on the monument offers the barest details of Fancher's life: "George Hicks Fancher. Born New York State February 9, 1828. Died in California March 30, 1900."

Travelers heading to and from Yosemite's Arch Rock entrance pass the Fancher monument every day. But, few, if any, ever stop to investigate the monolith rising out-of-place above the farmland. Henry had—the first time he left Yosemite via highway 140.

He was on foot then, and noticed the spire from a deceptive five miles away. The six-story plinth grew larger as Henry approached it, looming impressively in the two hours it took to walk there.

When he arrived, Henry took in the memorial as a whole—an obelisk atop a pyramid of stairs all surrounded by a low wall. He walked through an opening in the boundary of and onto the monument, up the ziggurat of stairs to read the inscription on the spire, then sat at the top of the steps and had lunch. He wondered who George Fancher was and what kind of life he had led to warrant such a large tribute in the middle of nowhere.

Henry had been to Yosemite several times but had never passed Fancher's self-dictated memorial. He'd never entered or exited the park on 140 and never before on foot. A month earlier, he'd parked his car somewhere—Henry no longer knew where—left it unlocked with his keys, wallet, and flip phone on the front seat, and walked away. Two-and-a-half-days and a 70-mile-walk later, Henry had been in the national park with no plans for the future or the then-present.

That was when Henry Lee and Earvin White first met, at a rocky stream near Yosemite's southern boundary. Earvin chanced upon Henry and, over the course of five days, saved him—though it was some time before Henry recognized that.

.

The second time Henry and Earvin met at Yosemite, three years later, Henry was two days late. Earvin had already been camped and fishing for a day, a night, and another day and night by the time Henry reached the lake.

"Henry, Henry, Henry," the older man said, "I wasn't sure you would make it." Earvin realized, as soon as he spoke, that he'd worried he wouldn't see the young man alive again. When they'd first happened upon each other, Henry had been on the verge of starvation and Earvin saw that the young man was burdened. With what—he'd not asked.

Henry said hello then spent a half-hour unpacking and setting up his tent before joining Earvin on the shore. They fished until early afternoon, made dinner from their catch, and camped overnight. Following that, the two hiked throughout the park's southern reaches for three more days before Mr. White, as he was known at school, had to return to the world of teaching and grading and the everyday turmoil of teenagers.

Throughout the trip, Earvin didn't ask Henry how he was or what he had done in the interval since their first meeting in Yosemite. He simply remarked, after he'd broken camp, that his friend—he considered Henry his friend—looked better than then.

"I stopped eating those terrible fruit and nut bars. Maybe that's it," Henry said.

"May be," said Earvin. He donned his worn pack full of clothing, camping, and fishing gear. "I'll see you again."

Henry nodded. "I'll be more punctual next time." He waved goodbye as Earvin started off into the woods on his way out of the park.

·

The third time Henry and Earvin met at Yosemite, another three years later, they arrived at the lake within a few hours of each other. Earvin arrived first, again, and was setting up a campsite as Henry hiked up.

Earvin grinned when he saw Henry. "How the hell are you, Henry Lee?" He was happy to see Henry again, without the trepidation for his friend's welfare that he'd felt before.

Henry set down his backpack. "I can't complain. Well, I won't complain, at least."

"Any small fish we catch," Earvin advised, "you tell your complaints to them before we throw them back."

For the next five days, the older black man and the younger Asian man fished, and hiked, and camped. They talked about the season and conditions in the park and how they differed from years past. Henry didn't volunteer what his life was outside of their triennial meetings and Earvin didn't ask. The intersection of Henry's and Mr. White's lives recurred only in this place for this short period of time.

Sitting outside their tents on the afternoon before they would part ways again, Henry asked, "Do you know the Fancher monument?"

Earvin processed the question for a moment. "I don't think so, what's that?"

"One minute," Henry said. He got up and went to his tent, unzipped the entrance and ducked in. He emerged a moment later with a small, leather-bound photo album. The album had just 12 leaves and accommodated one 4x6 photo per page. Henry flipped through the album, then handed it to Earvin.

The photo Henry had chosen showed George Fancher's stone obelisk on top of its pyramid of steps. The monument stood against a cloudy sky and aside from trees in the background, there was nothing else in the frame.

"After I left the park the first time we met," Henry said, "I saw this towering over the fields. It's off the side of the highway on the way to Merced."

"Can't say I've seen this," said Earvin. "Who was he?"

Henry cleared his throat before starting. "George Fancher was a local farmer and banker. He never married and never had children. It's not clear if he's buried under the monument or not."

"Doesn't matter," Earvin said. He handed the album back to Henry. "The memorial is proof of the time he spent on Earth whether his bones are there or not."

Henry wondered if Fancher would have agreed. "I think we all make our monuments. Your students are yours; proof of the time you've spent here on earth." Henry held up the album open to the photo of George Fancher's memorial. "More meaningful than this."

Earvin didn't immediately reply. "My students aren't my monument," he said. "Their education doesn't celebrate me.

"When I'm gone," he added, "I only hope I'll have done more right for this world than wrong."

Neither man said anything for a few minutes.

Afternoon was turning to early evening in Yosemite. Sunset caught on distant mountainsides was turning from gold to orange while the valley where Earvin and Henry had camped deepened in shadow.

"I also made a monument to myself," Henry said. "It's everywhere, but people don't know it." He considered the photo of Fancher's obelisk.

"When I realized what I had built, I tried to tear it down. It's not the monument I want to leave behind.

Henry smiled. "I'll tell you about it next time."

.

The fourth time Mr. White and Henry met at Yosemite, they didn't.

Henry arrived at the lake where, nine years prior, Earvin had showed him how to fish. It was a time when Henry had walked out on everything in his life and was on the verge of walking out on life itself. Mr. White would never acknowledge that his encounter with Henry had saved the young man. He'd say, instead, that over time Henry had saved himself. But, Henry knew otherwise.

After his third day of waiting at the lake, Henry packed up and hiked to the other spots he and Earvin had frequented in years past. On his fifth day in the park, Henry trekked back to the lake to camp one more night. The next morning, having seen no sign of Mr. White, Henry Lee headed back to the trailhead and his car.

It took five hours to hike back to Henry's dusty, orange Volvo. When he arrived, he put his heavy pack in the back of the wagon, then popped the hood to replace the distributor cap he had taken with him. He sat in the car for ten minutes, thinking, then drove out of Yosemite.

Two hours later, at the sole intersection in Tuttle, California, population 99, Henry pulled off of Highway 140 and parked across the road from the last acre of land once owned by George Fancher.

Henry studied Fancher's memorial from the open window of his car. It looked the same as the first time he saw it. Its size was still impressive.

Henry got out and crossed the road to the monument. He climbed the steps up to the obelisk and reread the inscription there. "Rest in peace, George Fancher," he thought to himself.

And, there, he noticed on the top step in front of him, a river rock. The stone was in a Ziploc bag—the size you would keep a sandwich in. The plastic bag was scratched and weathered from its seemingly needless service of protecting a rock from the elements.

Henry picked up the rock and the Ziploc with it. He opened the seal and took out the rounded, fist-sized piece of granite. Left in the bag was a square of folded paper. Henry took out the square and opened it—a sheet of logoed stationery from Yosemite Lodge at the Falls.

On the page was a long note written in black pen. The handwriting was loose and shaky and wandered across the page. It took some effort for Henry to decipher.

"Young Mr. Lee," the writing began, "I'm not sure why, but I feel this letter will find you, and I hope it finds you well."

The note, from Mr. White, apologized for missing his and Henry's next Yosemite meeting. It revealed Earvin's early onset dementia diagnosis and retirement from teaching. The note explained that Mr. White had tried to find Henry, but after reaching out to 50 incorrect Henry Lees, Earvin was counting on the memorial of George Fancher to get in touch with the right one.

The letter detailed Earvin's last visit to Yosemite—rushed in recognition of his decreasing physical and mental ability. Ten months before he and Henry would have met again, Mr. White made his last independent trip. No camping, fishing, or hiking, but Earvin had wanted to see Yosemite on his own one last time.

The note closed with, "Don't worry about this thing—this monument—you created. In time it'll matter as much as George Fancher's." It was signed at the bottom, "Your friend, Earvin."

Yosemite

S F O

"I LOVE AIRPORTS," Cynthia declared.

She and Andres were having lunch—her treat—in SFO's international terminal. Food options in the small, pre-security food court were a Japanese sushi/noodle bar, an Italian café, and Starbucks. Andres and Cynthia had both opted for panini and pasta salads from the café, although Cynthia ended up going to Starbucks for a latte over the Italian place's espresso bar. "I got a gift card for my birthday and haven't had a chance to use it," she explained.

Cynthia had invited Andres to the airport to see an installation of photography created with her startup's software. The exhibit consisted of a series of user-submitted photos shot with Cynthia's app—Rainbow.

"It's not my app," Cynthia complained. "If anything, it's Trang's app."

"You know what I mean," Andres said. He picked through his pasta salad looking for black olives. "What are you guys calling yourselves, anyway?"

Cynthia groaned. "Mission CZT." Then, she made a face. "It's supposed to be a placeholder name."

"I think you should go with Cynthia and Company," Andres ventured.

Cynthia laughed. "I don't think Zack and Trang would appreciate being 'and Company.'"

"Anyway, you haven't said what you think of the exhibit."

The exhibit—still being installed at the other end of the terminal— was a 22-foot wide by 8-foot high grid of photos created with Rainbow. The photos each featured the app's eponymous arc in the skies of various locales around the world: San Francisco, Paris, Sao Paolo, Capetown. The iOS app essentially did one thing—it let you put a virtual rainbow in the sky visible only by looking through your phone. You could then take a high-resolution photo of the scene.

"The rainbows were composited in-app?" Andres asked. "You didn't fix them in Photoshop?"

Cynthia confirmed that the rainbows were all app-generated, and Andres was impressed with their photorealistic quality.

Rainbow app, which was in closed beta, had 10,000 users. Cynthia was surprised at how quickly download requests had ramped up since they had launched via word-of-mouth—no media buys or even a press release. By the time word hit the tech and coolhunting blogs, Rainbow was near its maximum number of beta users.

"Someone commented to us that they really enjoyed Rainbow— that it made them happy," Cynthia said. "Whenever they're feeling down, they go outside and look through their phone for their rainbow." She put the plastic lid back on the remainder of her pasta salad. "Who would think you could get paid to make people pointlessly happy?"

"How are you getting paid, anyway?" Andres asked.

Cynthia & Co., which is how Andres was going to refer to the startup partnership no matter what, had almost run out of money. Instead, an 11th-hour backer had kept the company open by hiring them to develop Rainbow. The app arose from the ashes of an augmented reality feature from Cynthia, Zack, and Trang's shelved photosharing software.

"It's some guy that Trang worked with when he was still a Fed programmer," Cynthia said. "He heard that our photo app imploded, reached out to Trang, and contracted us to develop mobile AR software.

"Rainbow,"—Cynthia held up her phone so that Andres could see the Rainbow icon—"is the first of three apps."

Andres thought about this for a moment. "So, you have a new business partner?"

"No, we're being hired to do these projects, so he's not a partner. Otherwise, we'd have to change our name to Mission CZT-question-mark."

"Why question mark?"

"Question mark because I haven't met Mr. Moneybags or even learned his name."

.

Andres and Cynthia were back at the Rainbow photo exhibit on the opposite end of the International Terminal. With the installers done and cleared out, Cynthia was taking photos of the exhibit.

"I'm surprised you're not just using your iPhone," Andres remarked.

Cynthia stuck her tongue out at Andres, then walked her camera and tripod 30 yards away from the installation. Andres followed.

He watched as travelers walked past the grid of rainbow photos. A well-dressed Asian couple; a multi-generational, Tagalog-speaking family; a quartet of stereotypically Scandinavian college students—scores of people with their boarding passes, luggage, and multitude of dress. Most gave the wall of images a passing glance. A few, with time to spare before their flights, perhaps, took longer looks and read the text block describing the photography and its sources. Many took photos with their smartphones. Cynthia shot photos of them all, the shutter on her Nikon DSLR clicking away.

One boy, maybe seven or eight, running ahead of his parents and older sister, stopped and stared at the installation. When his family had passed him and then gotten some distance away, the parents sent the daughter back to retrieve her mesmerized brother.

"I've only been inside SFO once before," Andres said.

"Oh?" answered Cynthia, concentrating on the digital viewfinder on her camera's back.

"Actually, the only time I've been to an airport or flown is when my parents took us to Peru before my grandfather died. That was in 2000."

"Really?" said Cynthia. "How old were you?"

"12," Andres answered. "I imagine air travel now is different than then."

"Yeah, there's a ton of security, and the seats are 30-percent smaller or something." Cynthia straightened and looked at Andres. "Plus, you're probably 50-percent bigger than when you were 12.

"How can you not have flown anywhere in ten years?"

Andres shrugged. "It just hasn't happened. Any trip I've taken since then has been by car.

"Anyway, I like this airport energy. I may come here for lunch more often."

.

Andres watched a line of travelers snaking their way through security. He and Cynthia had returned to the food court and parked at a table so that Cynthia could download the photos she had taken from her camera to her laptop. She also went to the Starbucks counter for another latte, a piece of cake, and a mocha for Andres even though he hadn't asked for one. "I may burn through this gift card in one day," she said.

A man with a rolling backpack was arguing with a blue-uniformed security agent at the mouth of the maze leading to the TSA checkpoint. Andres couldn't hear the exchange between the two—the man repeatedly gestured to his backpack while the agent shook his head "no." Whatever it was, the Department of Homeland Security worker was not going to let this man into the line to have his person and belongings examined for threats. Thwarted, the angry traveler stormed off in the direction of the airline ticket counters.

"What was it that Trang did for the government?" Andres asked. "Maybe he was part of some elite cyberterrorism unit."

"He was a database programmer for the USDA or something." Cynthia took a sip of her third espresso drink of the day. "Can you imagine him as a hacker?"

Andres flashed on an image of Trang skateboarding through a server room, like Fisher Stevens in the terrible '90s movie *Hackers*.

.

Andres had watched *Hackers* one-and-a-half times on the second leg of his family's 14-hour journey to Peru. For the trip, his middle brother had bought a portable DVD player with an LCD screen, but neglected to bring any DVDs to watch. When the subject came up now, Andres' middle brother blamed their oldest brother for failing to bring the seven movies they had calculated necessary for their travel time.

During the family's two-hour layover at Miami International, 12-year-old Andres searched airport gift shops and found Florida travelogue DVDs and a single, $6-on-sale copy of *Hackers*. Interested in computers and unfamiliar with the movie, he excitedly brought the DVD to his parents to buy.

20 minutes into the flight from Miami to Lima, Andres and his middle brother, sitting on his left, split a pair of earbuds and started watching the movie. 50 minutes in, Andres was asleep. After waking two hours later, Andres watched the DVD all the way through, sharing the screen and earbuds with his oldest brother sitting on his right. As their plane began descending towards Lima's international airport, the brothers exchanged their views on *Hackers*.

Andres thought the movie was so-so but its depiction of computer programming and hacking was "really, really bad."

His oldest brother felt "the girl is pretty," but didn't like her short hair.

Andres' middle brother said the eldest was an idiot because "the girl is super-hot."

Andres felt the girl was beautiful but didn't say anything about it to his brothers.

In the end, the DVD and player were left in Lima with Andres' grandfather, who became fascinated by the device when he saw it in use. Andres later learned that his grandfather, who neither spoke English nor had ever used a computer, had watched *Hackers* over a dozen times in the months before he passed away. Even after Andres' Peruvian cousins had managed to circumvent the portable player's DVD region lockout, Andres' grandfather would watch *Hackers* with Spanish subtitles instead of playing actual Spanish-language discs.

·

"Did you know Angelina Jolie was in the movie *Hackers*?" Andres asked Cynthia. "I think my grandfather might have had a thing for her," he added.

To the parking structure

KILROY WAS HERE

"PINEAPPLE UPSIDE-DOWN CAKE," Dallas said abruptly.

"What?" asked Samantha from her neighboring cubicle.

Dallas pushed off from his desk and rolled away from his computer, spinning his office chair so that it faced Samantha's cube behind him. He expounded: "Whenever I was at a grocery store, I used to go to the baking goods aisle and flip the boxes of pineapple upside-down cake mix upside-down."

Samantha eyed Dallas in the mirror mounted on the side of her computer. "What?" she repeated.

"It was kind of a visual joke," Dallas explained.

Samantha pictured an inverted pineapple upside-down cake box. "I see," she said. "I guess."

"My girlfriend in college had the same reaction," Dallas said. "Her roommate, though, thought it was hilarious."

"And why, exactly, are you sharing your cake box hijinks with me now?" Samantha asked over her shoulder.

"I was just reading an article about memes and how the Internet amplifies their spread."

"Like 'I can haz cheezeburger'?" Samantha ventured.

"Sure," Dallas said, "though memes aren't solely an Internet phenomenon. The word was coined in the '70s to describe ideas that are spread culturally."

"Like 'I can haz cheezeburger.' " Samantha confirmed.

"Also advertising jingles, or fashion trends, or the idea of the tooth fairy, or the theory of relativity. All memes."

249

Samantha finally turned her chair around to face Dallas. "What does this all have to do with pineapple upside-down cake?"

Dallas recounted the main points of the article he'd been reading: smartphones and the Internet have accelerated the spread of memes; but, memes are not a new thing. Memes spread whenever an individual encounters new ideas. A parent telling their child to cover their cough or magazine readers learning a cooking tip both show the transmission of memes. Dallas' example was, "when a movie catchphrase becomes popular."

"I'll be back," Samantha said in the voice of Arnold Schwarzenegger's T-800.

"Exactly," said Dallas. "Anyway, I realized the upside-down pineapple cake box is a meme, too. When I was still in elementary school my brother saw it one day at Safeway. The next time we went to a grocery store he went to the cake mix shelves and flipped the pineapple upside-down boxes himself." Sometimes his brother would let Dallas flip the boxes and sometimes they would both flip one box—there were usually two. "We have no idea who started it, or if other people ever picked up on it."

"I'm not sure the upside-down cake box has what it takes to go viral," Samantha said. "Maybe if you put pictures of upside-down cats on the boxes instead."

"Doesn't matter," said Dallas. "It doesn't seem like the grocery stores I visit carry pineapple upside-down cake mix anymore. They only have pineapple supreme."

"Bummer," said Samantha. "If only the popularity of upside-down cake coincided with the rise of social media and smartphones."

"At least the meme has reached one more person," Dallas posited, "now that you know."

"Oh, no," Samantha answered. "I'm forgetting all about this as soon as I turn this chair around."

.

Amber stopped off at Kroger on her way home from the hospital. It was raining in Memphis, and thunderstorms were on the forecast for the next several days in eastern Tennessee and neighboring counties in Arkansas.

It had been a rough day at work and the weather fit her mood. Or, vice versa.

She started off in the produce aisle, picking up a sack of apples and, despite the calories, a couple of bananas. Amber considered three different types of head lettuce before opting for a pre-leafed, pre-washed package of mixed greens. She rounded out her salad plans with a bunch of carrots, a cucumber, and alfalfa sprouts.

Amber made one stop in the meat department for a package of boneless, skinless chicken breasts. If she were still alive, her grandma would have chided Amber for spending extra on cut-up and deboned poultry. She probably also would have faulted Amber for not slaughtering and plucking the bird herself. "This is why you don't have a husband," grandma would have told her. Amber losing weight when she went off to college in California would be another grandma-cited reason for her husbandless state.

Amber looked at her grocery choices and calculated that her entire cart totaled less calories than a typical Hardee's meal. In an unconscious nod to grandma, she made a decision.

"I'm going to bake a cake," Amber said. Then she thought, "Oh, God, I'm talking to myself out loud."

She headed to the baking goods shelves which were among the swath of store aisles that Amber had actively ignored for almost a decade.

Chips, cookies, and cereal were also on the verboten list. Her plan was to bake the cake, have a slice, feel better about how her day had gone, and then bring the rest of the cake to work.

Maybe she would just bring half of the cake to work. A cake missing one slice somehow seemed weird.

The cake mix shelves, which Amber had last visited during her sophomore year in college, seemed much the same as she had left them. One exception was red velvet cake mix, which she didn't remember from before. When did that become popular?

As Amber perused the various cake mix flavors, she saw a box which reminded her of how much fun she'd had in college. It had been hard, to be sure, moving across country and not knowing anyone. School, too, had been tough—her four years of undergrad were just as rigorous as the four years she spent on her PharmD.

But, Amber had met so many different, wonderful people at college and had so many adventures in her eight years in the Bay Area. Finding a pharma job back home right after graduation had seemed perfect, but two years later, her job was the only real thing left keeping her in Memphis.

She looked at the shelves full of brightly colored boxes and made another, bigger decision. "I'm going back to California," Amber said, quietly, to herself.

Then, she smiled, turned the box of pineapple upside-down cake mix upside down, and continued her way through the store.

The meat department

END OF THE RAINBOW

MIRANDA AND HER DAUGHTERS WERE SETTLING INTO THEIR ROOM at the Yosemite Lodge at the Falls. The room, on the second floor of a brown, two-story building, seemed to have been designed in and not remodeled since the 1960s. But, everything was tidy and clean and the snow on the balcony outside was a first-time thrill for Miranda's younger daughter.

.

Location, in part, had brought Miranda and her girls to Yosemite.

In the morning, Miranda had driven down from the Bay Area to Merced—gateway to Yosemite—and met her estranged husband who had driven up, with their two daughters, from Fresno. Situated between their respective homes, Yosemite was an opportune place for the family to meet not-quite-halfway.

Rather than hand off the children at a parking lot, Miranda's husband had suggested lunch at a pizza place he'd found online. The pizza turned out to be pretty good, and Miranda recognized, as the four of them sat and ate, that the last time they had a meal together had been over two years prior. To Miranda's youngest daughter it felt like it had been forever.

After pizza, Miranda said goodbye to her (still-)husband, bundled the girls into her new used car and headed to Yosemite Valley. The two-hour drive on highway 140 took them out of the small town of Merced straight through surrounding farms and then steadily wound up and down into forest, hills, and river valleys. The open farmland sky was gradually replaced by tree canopy as they drove into Stanislaus National Forest and then under the Arch Rock entrance to Yosemite National Park. As they entered Yosemite Valley the sky returned, in breathtaking fashion, opening up above the massive rock face of El Capitan.

Miranda pulled over and parked, and she and her daughters got out of the car to gaze across a broad meadow at the 3,500-foot-tall rock formation. They took photos of the distant granite wall, the snow-covered field and surrounding trees, and each other.

Miranda's eldest snapped away with her secondhand Olympus digital SLR. The camera was a recent birthday gift from her mom and dad. In turn, Miranda's youngest had inherited from her sister use of the family's compact digital camera. The Canon point-and-shoot replaced the 7-year-old's pretend camera that had been made from a found mint tin. The little girl took photos of the mountain and clouds and interesting leaves she saw and a small snowman she and her mom built.

Miranda's camera was her smartphone. She photographed the scenery and her daughters—mostly her little one. She managed to get her girls to pose together for one photo though her eldest refused to smile. The teenager otherwise hid her face whenever Miranda tried to take her picture. She had to sneak photos when the 16-year-old wasn't looking.

Miranda's eldest snuck a photo, as well, of her mother and her little sister playing in the snow. Years later, Miranda would see the photo for the first time framed and on the wall of her eldest's apartment. Looking at it, she would recall this trip as a bright spot during a difficult period in her relationship with her daughter.

After El Capitan, the trio stopped twice more as the drive took them to views of Half Dome and Yosemite Falls. There were majestic scenes to stop for everywhere throughout the valley—enough to delay their arrival at their hotel. They ended up checking in much later than planned.

In their cozy, '60s-decorated room that night, Miranda and her daughters ate their leftover pizza for dinner and went to bed as new snow started falling in the valley.

.

Photography, in large part, had brought Miranda and her girls to Yosemite.

Miranda's older daughter had a keen interest in and growing aptitude for taking photographs. She had never been to Yosemite, but the 16-year-old was familiar with Ansel Adams' landmark views of the national park. She had studied Adams' Yosemite photos in her high school photography class and had been excited—though she'd tried to act blasé—when her mom said they would be visiting the park. The teenager wanted to experience firsthand the iconic scenes that Adams had captured and visit the Ansel Adams Gallery in Yosemite Valley.

Miranda, too, wanted to visit the national park and see in person views that she had come to know from photographs. The images Miranda was familiar with though, were far from famous. The photos of Yosemite that she knew were from a virtual unknown—Henry.

Henry's photos of snow-covered Yosemite were in black-and-white—different from his color images of the Pacific Northwest, Southern California, and Hawaii. Only two of his Yosemite pictures were of landmarks—El Capitan and Glacier Peak. The other four were of frozen forest, fields, and ponds. There were no people in the photos. Not the young woman, who was often the subject of Henry's other photos, nor Henry, who appeared only once in a self-portrait with the young woman.

Miranda had never met Henry, but she had formed an idea of who he was from his photography. Henry's photos had come to Miranda by chance. Some would credit fate, but not Miranda, at least not for herself. She thought of fate as something for other people.

Miranda's youngest daughter didn't yet understand the concept of fate. When the then-six-year-old found a plastic-wrapped mint tin partially unearthed beneath a tree, she didn't assume that she had been destined to find it. When the tin was revealed to have a digital memory card inside, Miranda's daughter took that to be an everyday extraordinary occurrence. In her mind, random important things were available to be found by anyone anytime.

Andres—Miranda's co-worker who had discovered that the memory card held photos, and then downloaded, reconstructed, and printed them—didn't consider the scenario to be fateful. The buried memory card was just mysterious—a riddle to be solved. Andres and his tech friends searched the card, tin, and card's digital files for clues but came up empty. As far as they could tell, the unearthed memory card wasn't a geocache prize or a clue in an alternate reality game. Thus far, the puzzle proved to be un-Googleable. Searches either turned up hundreds of mundane results—'DIY memory card case,' 'photographer Henry'—or zero relevant results—'.lee file format,' 'buried treasure Fresno county.' Reverse image searches didn't match any of the 22 photos recovered from the card.

Madeline, who had identified for Miranda the mystery photographer, thought the whole story was awesome. What were the odds that she would be seated with Henry for dinner on a train trip with her dad and then years later meet Miranda who was looking at a stack of photos that had Henry in it? "What an amazing chain of circumstances," she messaged her best friend Aaron. "Life is a chain of circumstances," he sent back. "You're an un-amazing chain of circumstances," she replied. Aaron responded with ":-P".

Miranda's teenage daughter didn't imagine that the hand of fate had brought Henry's photos to light. But, she did consider that the photos themselves might have wanted to be seen. The images, trapped on a memory card in a small box under a tree, somehow made themselves found by the teen's younger sister. Her little sister then carried the box around for months before giving it to their mom, who found the memory card and then gave it to someone who could decipher the photos and have them printed. It was like a Japanese horror movie where an evil video compels people to watch it and then kills them.

Henry's photos weren't scary, though. Most of them just felt lonely. Maybe that's why they wanted to be seen.

.

Over the next three days, Miranda drove close to 300 miles throughout the park. On the first day, she and the girls drove to the Hetch Hetchy reservoir and, on the way back to the lodge, to Crane Flats. The next day, they took the Tioga Road to Tuolumne Meadows. Their third driving trip took them to the Mariposa Grove near the park's southern border.

Miranda knew, logically, how large Yosemite was, but she hadn't realized how much time they would be spending in the car. The drives, while scenic, were at least an hour each way and proved to be a good time for Miranda's seven-year-old to snooze before dinner. By the third day of driving, walking, and hiking, the car ride back to the lodge was nap time for both of Miranda's daughters.

After driving up, down, and all around the park, Miranda and her daughters spent their last day-and-a-half traveling solely on foot in Yosemite Valley.

.

Technology, ultimately, had brought Miranda and her girls to Yosemite.

Some months ago, Miranda's co-worker Andres had stopped by to see if everything was working out with Miranda's new smartphone. Miranda replied, "Yes," and said how amazed she was at the number of things she did with the phone. She had never utilized her previous cellphone—or computer for that matter—to the extent that she used her iPhone now.

Andres asked if Miranda had heard of an app called "Rainbow." She hadn't. "What is it?" she asked.

"It's an augmented reality app that puts a virtual rainbow in the sky," Andres explained. "Do you have time to go outside? It would be easier to show you."

Downstairs, amid the sidewalk traffic along Market Street, Andres held his phone up in front of him, as if he were taking a picture of the sky. He panned his camera view down the long corridor of buildings headed southwest towards the Castro and Bernal Heights.

"There," he said. Andres handed his phone to Miranda. "Look up and to the right. Can you see it?"

Miranda looked at Andres' iPhone screen. It showed the street behind as if the phone was a windowpane. She moved the screen's view until she could see "it" far off in the distance behind the buildings along Market Street—the rising arc of a rainbow.

·

Andres emailed Miranda a beta code for Rainbow app. He explained that the iOS app had been recently updated but was still not openly available. Andres was friends with the developers who were creating the app and had been given several download codes to share.

"You pick the ends of your rainbow," Andres wrote, "by inputting the far end—your goal. The other end is placed wherever you are when you pick the far end." He reiterated that there were two big changes in the updated version of Rainbow. First, you could now use a photograph to choose the distant end of your rainbow. The software would search for embedded location data in photos, and failing that, would attempt to image search for similar photos with location metadata. Second, once a rainbow was made, you couldn't change it. Your rainbow would persist until you reached the other end.

"Where does your rainbow go to?" Miranda had asked as she stood on Market street looking through Andres' iPhone.

"It goes from my parents' house to Hawaii," he answered. "I'm hoping to take them there next year."

That afternoon, Miranda sat at her small kitchen/dining table in her Richmond apartment. She thought about where she might make a rainbow to. What goal did she want to commit to a personal, virtual rainbow?

"I'd like to take the girls to Seattle," Miranda thought.

She launched Rainbow on her phone, which opened to a screen of blue sky with wispy white clouds. An input box at the top of the screen read "Search for a place or event." Miranda poised her finger to tap in the search box, then paused. Next to the input box was a small icon that looked like two photographs. She tapped on the photo icon which prompted her to select an image from her iPhone's camera roll. She swiped through the grid of thumbnails until she found the photograph she wanted.

In the photo, a young man is being kissed on the cheek by a young woman. The man, Henry, is taking the self-portrait with the camera held at arm's length. In the background are the Space Needle and downtown Seattle.

Of Henry's 22 photos, Miranda considered this the first one. It was the beginning of a story told in images that had been hidden from sight in a peppermints box beneath a tree in the San Joaquin Valley.

She selected the photo which expanded to fill the screen. After a moment, the image dimmed to accommodate a superimposed message.

"We've located the end of your rainbow." Beneath the message, two buttons appeared: Preview; and, Confirm.

Miranda tapped 'Preview' and the darkened image changed to the top of her kitchen table, as if the phone had turned transparent.

She put on her coat to go outside to inspect her rainbow. She walked out to her apartment complex's parking area, then took her phone out of her pocket. Through her iPhone's screen, Miranda saw a brilliant rainbow erupting out of the top of her building. She held her phone up above her head to follow the arc up into the sky and stretching away into the distance. She smiled and clicked the 'Confirm' button on the screen.

Miranda put her phone away, then realized something odd—the direction she was facing was not north towards Washington state. It was east.

She took her phone out again, relaunched the app and followed the rainbow from her building up into the clouds to the east. She could see the colored bands fading off in the distance past buildings and treetops and the horizon beyond Richmond. Miranda put her phone away, and, thinking for a moment, guessed where her rainbow led to.

.

On their last day in the park, Miranda and her two girls visited the Ansel Adams Gallery for a photography class and walk. Afterwards, they looked through an exhibit of Adams' prints and photo equipment. Miranda had to coax her teen to leave so that they could go eat lunch.

Miranda and her girls sat outside in their winter coats and hats at a covered patio table. The deck where they were situated had been swept, but there was snow piled on the rigid umbrella above their table. They ate cold sandwiches and drank hot cocoa.

For the first time since arriving at the park, Miranda took out her phone and launched the Rainbow app. She panned her phone around until she found her rainbow. The start end, some 150 miles away at her apartment in Richmond, was not visible. The finish end, though, was not far off from where they were sitting. Miranda's rainbow descended from the sky and disappeared into the wood-shingled roof of a two-story building. A red sign hung over the entrance to the rustic stone and wooden structure. It read, simply, MUSEUM.

.

Miranda stood in the Yosemite Museum gallery, separate from the museum's displays of Yosemite Valley geology, geography, and Native American life. The gallery was showing an exhibition of Yosemite-inspired art—art primarily by local artists, a sign at the entrance of the gallery read.

There were pieces in charcoal, pencil, watercolor, clay, glass, and wildflower collage depicting Yosemite's landmarks, flora, and fauna. A modern dance performance, playing on a flatscreen monitor, interpreted the effect of fire and winter storms on the park and its inhabitants.

A row of photos lined the back wall of the gallery. Most were in color—images of Tunnel View at sundown, a waterfall lit up like lava, El Capitan crowned with clouds. The photos were beautiful, but unable to convey the magnitude of their subjects. Miranda wondered if it was simply because they were smaller.

Smaller still, at the end of the row of brilliant color photos there were two black-and-white prints arranged one above the other. Miranda recognized them—the feeling of them—though she hadn't seen them before.

The image on top was round. Miranda's teenage daughter later explained that the spherical shape and distortion were from a fisheye lens. In the photo, a large tree, bare of leaves, stands in the middle of a

263

snow-dusted field. Some distance away, evergreens fade into the mist and mountains behind them.

The bottom photo, also taken in the winter, was rectangular and featured two figures by a lake. The two men wear cold weather gear and are posed for the camera. The man on the right, older and black, is seated on a folding camp chair. He sits slightly hunched over but cranes his neck to look straight into the camera. The younger man on the left stands with his hand on his seated companion's shoulder. Older in this photo than in his self-portrait from Seattle, the younger man is Henry.

A museum label beneath the two photos read:

h.lee

ABOVE

Tree in winter, 2010

Photographic print

BELOW

Mr. White, 2010

Photographic print

...

AFTERWORD

THE STORIES IN *HENRY AND MIRANDA* are fiction, but I hope they ring true to you.

The photos accompanying the stories are not always the places encountered by Henry, Miranda, and the rest. But, in most cases, the photos were the genesis of the stories. In a few instances, the words came first and then I looked for a photo or photo opportunity to match.

I started writing about Henry and Miranda three years ago on Backspaces, a mobile app and story-publishing platform. *Henry*, originally *When Henry Returned Home*, was a 75-word photo caption and the first fiction I had written since high school. Some weeks later, a series of pictures taken on BART inspired me to post *Miranda*. All told, I published 21 fiction pieces on Backspaces, almost half of what became this book.

The tool that Backspaces founders Adrian Sanders and Dmitri Cherniak created got me to write again. Thanks, guys.

—Calixto

Made in the USA
Monee, IL
28 September 2019